BACK TO O'GALLAGHERS: *Jake*

MIGNON MYKEL

BACK TO O'GALLAGHERS: Jake

MIGNON MYKEL

Jake
Drunk Girl

Colie
Thinking 'Bout You

Shayne
One Number Away

Saint
Alone Tonight

Ben
Going 'Round

Nick
Alone Tonight
...you don't meet him in Drunk Girl

Back to O'Gallaghers *is an interconnected, standalone series where each couple's story can be read without reading the other books. However, to get the most out of these friends and relationships, it is recommended to read in order.*

PREFACE

Because it may confuse some people, *Drunk Girl* takes place the March/April right before *Butterfly Save* (which starts around June of the same year)—so yes, Jonny is still in the goal.

Also, yes, that means you'll get some Enforcers references in here, too!

Happy reading!

ONE

Jake

Mid-March

"WELCOME TO O'GALLAGHERS," I mumble to no one, unlocking the back entryway to the Irish-American pub I've been working at for the better part of a year. We're not supposed to open solo, but my opener, Ben—who also happens to be my roommate—is making a run to the grocery store down the street for limes at the suggestion of last night's closer. It's better I sent him now; we won't get a third body in the pub for another two hours, and by that time, our kitchen order should be arriving. Once the truck comes we'll have other things to worry about.

It's not like this area is riddled with crime. It's a pretty safe neighborhood.

I do, however, lock the door behind me as I move into the kitchen.

My first tasks this morning include a preliminary check of the pub, which I do as I make my way to the alarm system. Nothing seems amiss.

Next to do? Inventory.

Beyond checking stock in the back and where we keep kegs, I do a quick visual sweep of the bar area. When Ben gets here with the limes, he'll prep and refill the condiment bar but I double-check that the only thing we needed from the store was limes. Inventory and setting up will take the majority of my time but I know, at about ten minutes before unlocking the door for the day, I'll need to get the register till in place. There's a fifteen minute time-delay to open the safe and remove the till, but I've been opening twice a week for the last eleven months. I have my tasks down to a science and know precisely when to set the safe for opening.

It's not long before there's a pounding that directs my attention to the front. The main door to the pub is old and wooden, with frosted glass in the top half. I don't know that it's original to the building, but it's been in place as long as the O'Gallagher family's been here.

Unlatching the set of locks, I open the door wide, allowing Ben in.

"How many d'you grab?" I ask, resecuring the locks.

"Just four." Ben tosses the bag on the bar, then ties his hair up in "man bun" at the top of his head.

I've been giving him shit about the hair for the last year.

Ben and I met a few months after I started at O'Gallaghers—he took a position shortly after I did. He needed a place to stay and I'd recently had a roommate move out.

Worked out great.

Worked out even better that he's an all-around good guy and easy to get along with.

That, and the fact we keep very similar schedules.

The guy's *only* negative is he's a modern day Snow White and the stray cats at our apartment complex gravitate toward him. Now my dog Boo, a mostly-white American Bully mix, herds cats around the apartment and has given up her extra-large bed for a blind, white cat named Sully.

"Figured the order is due to come today, isn't it? So, more will be here in time for the St. Paddy's shit." Ben is now behind the bar, washing his hands as he gets ready to cut and prep the condiments.

"Hopefully." The truck drivers have been arriving later than usual. They used to arrive right when we unlocked the doors but the last few weeks they haven't gotten here until closer to three. That's four hours to potentially be low—or worse, out—of something. And with only two or three bodies in the pub, if it's busy it's not easy to send someone to the store. Hence, sending Ben before we arrived here today.

While he has the front of house, I head into the office to start unlocking the safe and get the back of house ready. Fifteen minutes later, the till is in place and the day has officially begun.

Early afternoons aren't typically busy here, unless it's a sport day. Everyone in town knows that the NHL Enforcers hang out here and regardless of time, we have their games on live. We turn on baseball and football, too—hard no to golf, sorry not sorry; I'll play it, just can't get me to watch it —and the occasional NASCAR race on Sundays, but when it's not a sport day, it usually takes a while before people start piling in.

We'll probably see a few regulars that come in for lunch, and then the afterwork crowd will start walking through the doors at about three or so.

On days I work the late shift—six to two, although I've done some three to twos—the afterwork crowd starts to grow with the after dinner crowd, and then you have the late-nighters.

I don't know that there's a shift I prefer working the most, although it's nice to be able to go to bed before midnight on occasion.

Today's shift goes by easily, if not a little slow. We go up to three bartenders at two, and Shayne arrives right on time. She started at O'Gallaghers after Ben and me, but she's a hit with the regulars and when it was time for her or Ben to promote to shift lead, she was the one who got the position —not that Ben wanted it.

Everyone loves her. The majority of our staff is male, but whenever Shayne or our other female bartender Nicole —but goes by Colie—work, tips go up. They're fun when they work together—kind of good cop, bad cop vibes, with Colie being the good cop and Shayne being the bad.

We aren't the place to go to if you're looking for slutty barmaids, so it's not ass cheeks and titties that have people loving them. It's just their overall personalities.

Honestly, the group we have right now is great.

Usually when the nights get busier, Shayne works the floor more than behind the bar but today she'll stay at the bar so I can work on manager-type duties before I clock out for the day.

It's three now and I have all of my tasks completed. I can hear the growing crowd in the pub as well as the cook singing along to the small radio he keeps near his station, but before I can leave I need the three o'clock bartender to clock in and I haven't seen him yet.

I head out of the office and check on our cook, Pete— he's being kept busy with wings and fries today, but that's pretty normal for this time of day—before walking through the swinging door into the real hustle and bustle of O'Gallaghers. I'm not at all surprised to see a few high tops with customers and nearly every seat at the bar itself is taken. Looks like a normal Thursday night here. It's only going to get busier.

We're also heading into St. Patrick's Day weekend and the O'Gallaghers, being second generation Irish-Americans, do the holiday big.

"Hey, anyone see Travis?" I ask as both Shayne and Ben work on drinks and getting orders out. Ben is mostly running the floor because Shayne is the next shift lead.

"Nope, but can't say I'm surprised," Shayne mumbles, pouring a glass of Guinness from tap. She places the curved glass on a serving tray that Ben won't use.

"What do you mean by that?" A customer at the end of the bar holds up two fingers before she can clarify and I skirt around her to assist.

"Whiskey double," he orders, pushing his shot glass toward me. "Redbreast 15."

"Sure thing." I take the used shot glass, discarding it in the sink, before pouring him a double of the 15-year old aged whiskey. It's not the cheapest in the pub but judging by the man's Gucci sports jacket, he's not going to care.

Briefly, I wonder if he asked for it or if Shayne upsold him.

I'm leaning in the Shayne angle.

After I serve the guy, I walk back to the blonde with the forearm tattoo. Part of me thinks random men come into the pub and listen to her recommendations because she looks like a badass, but if you ask me, she's a marshmallow. When Ben trapped his first two cats, she said she'd help bring them to the vet—and then ended up keeping both.

Not that keeping two cats makes her a softy but I think

she has a hard front on purpose. What that purpose is, I haven't figured out.

"So. Travis?" I start to rinse glasses and put them in the underbar glasswasher.

"Yeah, some things he was saying his last shift led me to believe he wasn't going to show up this weekend. Like, he was going to be going out and enjoying the festivities."

I can't help but sigh. It's one of the craziest weekends we'll have at O'Gallaghers and the last thing we need is a new hire peacing out. "Let me go call him. You're good? Ben's here until four and then Saint comes in."

"I'm good. Go."

Leaving her to the front, I hit the swinging door and move into the back of house. "You good?" I ask Pete as I walk past him.

"Good. Chris comes in at five, yeah?"

"I believe so. I think both Chris and Hank."

"Oh. Yeah. You're right. Hank is prepping for the weekend. You think it's cool if I take my lunch when they get here?"

"I don't see a problem with that but I'll run it past Shayne in a minute. She's taking over the shift. I'm sure there won't be any issues, though."

Once in the office, I pull up the staff list on the computer and find Travis's information, dialing his number on the business phone. It rings in my ear five times before moving into his voicemail. "Hey, it's Jake," I tell the machine, even though based on Shayne's testimony, the effort is futile. "You're on the schedule for three. Just wondering if you're on your way. Give us a call. Thanks." Shaking my head, I press the phone base's hook-switch instead of putting the receiver down to hang up, then dial Conor's number by memory.

"This is Conor," he answers on the second ring.

"Hey, it's Jake. Travis was supposed to come in at three and hasn't. I called him, no answer. Shayne said that she's not surprised he no-showed. Normally, I'd call someone else in, but I know this weekend is all-hands-on-deck and I'm pretty sure almost everyone is bordering overtime."

My boss groans on the other end and I hear his mumbled "shit" beneath his breath. "Yeah. Fuck. Shit." So much for the mumbled one, I think with a chuckle. "All right, um... Turn down the T.V. for a second, Aiden. Please." His tone changes between talking to his oldest, and talking to me. Not many expect the bearded, tattooed man to be a softy with his family. "*Fuck.* Of all days for Brenna and Stone to be in freaking Arizona." Brenna is Conor's sister, and she and her husband, Stone—former bartender, now part of the overall business team—are in Arizona with their kids visiting the third O'Gallagher, Rory, and *his* wife and their kids. "Look, I'll come in, but is there any way you can stay until I get there? Mia's on day three of the flu, and I'm pretty sure the girls are down with it now too. It's been hell here but I can't get them into the pediatrician until tomorrow. Thank fuck they have morning open clinic hours because we're going to be swamped this weekend. Let me see if I can send Aiden somewhere for the night and get the estrogen in the house settled." It sounds like the man is stressed. I don't blame him. "It might be seven, eight before I get there though. I don't really want Mia out of bed and dealing with the girls. She damn near passed out walking downstairs this morning. But fuck, I know that's a long fucking day for you. You're not on the schedule tomorrow, right?"

"I'm not. It's not a big deal, I'm happy to stick around."

"Thank you. I fucking knew that kid was no good but I

went against my better judgement. All right. I'll try calling him but I'm sure I'll get the same response you did. Thanks, Jake."

I walk back to update Shayne, also giving her the heads up that Pete needs a lunch when the other two cooks come in. With that, I hand over the shift-managerial duties to her. I'm more than happy doing grunt work for the next few hours.

As predicted, the crowd starts to pick up as five rolls around. I like it busy, especially on hour seven of my day. Ben's clocked out now, leaving Shayne, Saint, Colie, and myself on the floor.

"I am *not* in the mood for a bachelorette party," Saint groans, popping tops off glass beer bottles.

Frowning, I look in the direction of his gaze and see a party of seven females, all wearing black tank tops with something written over their chests. One is wearing a silver sash.

March in San Diego isn't *exactly* tank top weather, especially as the sun goes down, but to each their own.

"You know they'll tip better if one of you boys helps them," Colie replies, sliding an order sheet across the smooth maple bar top.

Where Shayne is rough edges, Colie is girl next door. If either of the girls would be able to work with a group of women, it would be Colie, but she does have a point. A small group of two or three women, they usually respond better having one of the girls. But a large group...

Yeah, she's not wrong.

"Fine. I'll take 'em," I say, tapping the bar twice with the side of my fist before walking toward the group. They pulled two high tops together, splitting both Colie's and my sections. As I near, I see their shirts draw attention to the fact it's someone's birthday.

Probably Sash Girl.

"Hey, ladies," I say, stepping between a dark-blonde and a redhead, laying cocktail napkins on the tables. "My name's Jake. What brings you in tonight?"

Sash Girl smiles and lifts both hands in the air. "It's my birthday!" Most of the party echoes, "It's her birthday!" as if this isn't the first birthday celebration they've done as a collective.

"We're doing a pub crawl and decided to start here," Birthday Sash Girl announces, leaning into the table. "It's gonna be a good night, right girls?" More echoing happens, but I notice the blonde to my left isn't as echo-y as the rest of the group.

She's participating, but not at the same decibel as the others.

"Well, happy birthday to you. I'm going to venture to guess it's not the big twenty-one, but I'll still need to see some IDs, regardless if you're ordering alcohol or not."

"Oh. We are *definitely* ordering alcohol tonight," the woman to Birthday Sash Girl's left declares.

Some of the ladies have clutch purses, some have card holders that are attached to their phones, but every one of them has a driver's license on them. Once I'm sure each party goer is legal—Birthday Sash Girl, legal name Megan, is turning twenty-five tomorrow and most of the group is around the same age—I take their drink order.

At the moment, they're only interested in shots.

"I'll be right back," I tell the group, leaving them for the bar.

"Bachelorette?" Saint asks, shaking a cocktail.

"Birthday. And twenty-five," I add, with a shake of my

head. Twenty-one? Yeah. Thirty? Could see it. You ask me, and twenty-five is just another birthday—but what do I know? I just serve the alcohol.

Lining up seven shot glasses, I expertly pour the tequila Megan asked for down the row. Once all are filled, I place them on a serving tray and move back through the growing crowd.

This time when I approach the group, I move to stand between Megan and the friend who was "definitely ordering alcohol tonight."

Lisa, I think her name was.

Mostly because across from them is the light-haired, softer-spoken one of the group.

Sophia.

As I pass out the shots of tequila, I make sure to make eye contact with each woman—girls like when we do—and when it's time to place the seventh shot glass in front of Sophia, I wait for her to lift her eyes.

And am immediately taken aback by the hazel depths.

"All right, ladies," I say, my eyes remaining locked with the soft-spoken one. "Here's your first round."

"Aw, you should've brought one for you!" Megan says, leaning into me. Her perfume is stronger than I prefer on a woman.

Probably so it lingers all night, masking the smell of alcohol and sweat.

"How about you bring us a second round, but do one with us?" Megan asks, putting her hand on my forearm. I glance down at her French manicured claws.

That's exactly what they are. They're filed to sharp points.

It's against California law to drink while serving, although there is a loophole that says we can taste to ensure we're serving quality drinks. I've always thought that loop-hole was more meant for the wineries that bring tourists to the state, and never sought to test my luck.

"Sorry, ladies, not tonight," I say, pulling my arm from under her hold. When she moves her hand to my ass, I fight the urge to tell her off.

"You enjoy yourselves, though." I leave the group, hearing their exclamations before shooting their shots back, and inform Colie that she can bring the next round.

I'm not above flirting with patrons but I don't enjoy being pawed at, and that Megan is a pawer.

"Are you afraid of a bunch of girls?" Colie teases, watching as I line up the next set of tequila shots.

"Nope, not at all, but I'm also not in the mood to be eye-fucked and fondled."

Colie bursts out laughing. "Oh, you're a hoot, Jake Wesley."

Years before, well before I started, the pub put in place a very firm No Touching rule, but it mostly applied to the male patrons and the female staff. We get the occasional new guy who wanders in and breaks the rule but they learn pretty quickly that it isn't tolerated.

Our group—Travis aside—is like a small family unit and you don't mess with family.

After Colie sends over the next round of shots, she comes back to close the group out.

"Already?" I ask, wiping down a section of bar after a patron left. Maybe I made a mistake in not personally sending the second set of shots over. It's never a good thing when a larger group is only in the building for ten minutes.

"I've been informed they have five more places to hit. Gonna be a long night for them." Colie chuckles as she closes out the tab, printing out the check.

It's only a few minutes more before the group heads toward the exit, Megan in front and Sophia in the back. I watch as they leave through the door—and I don't bother examining why I have to force myself to pull my gaze away from the last woman of the pack.

TWO

Sophia

I'M NOT REALLY the "go out and drink" type.

One, I'm a lightweight compared to my friends and have been since the first time we drank together. Two, I've never really seen the point in getting so wasted you're in physical pain the next day. And then finally, there's three; if I ever *do* want to drink, I'd much rather partake while in my comfies, lounging on my oversized couch, sipping a red while watching whatever latest movie is streaming on any of my numerous apps.

Nights like tonight aren't a "sip and savor your drink" kind of night, which means I'll have to fake or pace.

Regardless of which I choose, some of these girls are known to get sloppy—and with sloppy comes loud and embarrassing. I suppose it would be more bearable if I was drunk, too, but then again, I've never been able to block the constant wheel of wondering what others see or think when they look at me. The irritating desire to be what they need me to be, never turning off.

People pleaser at her finest, right here. All I need to complete the look is flashing neon lights.

Which is how I found myself downtown on a Thursday night for a bar crawl, celebrating Megan's birthday. Aside from my roommate, Emina, I haven't hung out with the entire group of girls in a few months and all six of them took turns in making me feel like I was a party pooper for not wanting to come out tonight. As a collective, we celebrate everyone's birthdays and have since our first year in college.

We're only three bars in—of seven—and I know this night is going to take a lot out of me. It already has. With the mental drain of fake smiles and false pretenses, I'm dreading what the next half hour will bring as more alcohol is poured and passed around the table.

I'm your classic introvert. I need quiet and solitude to recharge, and while I don't mind going out with my closest friends, as one hour drags into two, it starts to take its toll.

It's a good thing we decided to walk tonight—these girls don't seem to give two flying shits about how much alcohol they're consuming, and I'm pretty sure Megan and at least two others are wasted already.

I took one shot at the first place but then faked the second round. No one noticed that my glass wasn't empty when I placed it back down. They were all more excited to move on to the next stop.

Then the next.

Where we're at now, the music is so loud, the bar may as well be a club.

As an old Justin Timberlake song comes on and the bass drops, my friends begin to scream in excitement. I plaster a smile on my face and rock my hips, pretending to enjoy myself when all I really want to do is go home.

People Pleaser Sophia will probably be out with the girls all night.

Mostly because I don't know how to say, "Hey, I'm leaving. Have fun." I could turn to Emina and get her to make excuses for us. Everyone knows she prefers to be in bed when the sun goes down. Glancing over at her though, her dancing and singing looks legit.

She's having fun.

"All right!" Lisa yells over the music, re-securing her brown hair in a cute messy bun. "Megan. If you could have *anything*... AN.NY.THING. Anything at all. For your birthday tomorrow... What would you like?"

"A trip to Paris, would be my answer," Shaina giggles, bringing her cocktail to her lips and sipping through the tiny straw.

Megan points to her, grinning. "Not a bad wish! Not. A. Bad. *Wish!*"

"But totally better if you brought all of us along, amiright?" comes from another of our friends, Jane.

"Totally," Megan grins.

This whole night feels like we're back a few years and celebrating Emina's twenty-first birthday. Has no one grown up? Okay, that's a little harsh. Emina's probably just as easy to convince to stay in as I am. We make great roommates.

Megan is the oldest of our group, with Em being the youngest. In college, we did our birthdays in our sorority house but when it was Emina's turn to turn legal, we went out and partied hard.

Tonight is literally that night all over again, down to the silver birthday sash, the over-exaggerated giggles and jokes, and the shots after shots after shots.

"Bu-u-u-u-ut..." Megan draws out. "If I could have *anything* at all?" She looks down at the table, picking up her fruity mixed drink. Then, with a sly smile on her face and the rim of her glass near her mouth, she says, "I'd totally corner Josh Pine and have my filthy way with him."

Everything in me stills.

Because Josh Pine—

"*Sophia's* Josh?" Em asks beside me, leaning into the table as if she misheard our friend. The level of disbelief in her voice isn't hard to miss.

Megan doesn't look at me but instead, she moves her eyes to look at Shaina. Thanks to her natural red hair, Shaina blushes easily and looks uncomfortable with the glance.

Like she's guilty of something.

My head is a jumble of words but I can't get any of them out.

"What the fuck, Megan?" *Thank God for Em.*

The seven of us may have gone to college together, but Em has been my friend since we were paired together Freshman year. We went from college dorms to the sorority house to a townhouse just a few miles away from here, best friends since eighteen. I may not see the others very often, but Em always has my back.

"I mean..." Megan looks at me this time, shrugging her shoulder. "It's not like you guys are exclusive."

Jaw dropping, I'm immediately taken aback. "What do you mean, we're not exclusive? I'm fucking dating him, am I not?"

"You're not *fucking* him," my supposed friend rolls her eyes.

How in the hell would they know that? Besides...she's mostly wrong. Josh and I have been dating a little over two months and sure, we've only had sex once, but he's come to at least two get-togethers as my plus-one. At some point or another over the time he and I have been seeing one another, he's met every single one of them—*while with me.*

"What does that even matter?" Em stands up for me, once again.

"Shaina fucked him first!" Jane blurts out, before pushing her shoulders up and her chin down, like a turtle trying to retreat into a shell.

"What?!" I shriek—not my finest moment—swinging my head to look at the redhead I'd considered to be my second best friend in the group, behind Em.

Emina grabs hold of my forearm, not that I'm going to launch myself at Shaina.

Her face is still flushed from her earlier blush, but she has the nerve to shrug a shoulder and say with a straight face, "He told me you aren't willing to put out."

I can't stop my jaw from dropping open. He told her that? All because I told him after our first time together that I needed us to pump the breaks just a little? I'm not usually one to give into passionate flings, but he'd been attractive and attentive, and I'd been single for a bit longer than I cared for...

Kissing lead to the bedroom faster than I could say, "Yes," and I felt a little gross about myself the morning after.

Besides...

It wasn't like he'd been asking for sex and I was telling him no. It just...

Hasn't come up since I told him I needed us to slow down a little.

I should have realized it hadn't "come up" because someone else was getting it up for him.

"Look, Soph," Lisa butts in, "guys have needs. We all

know you're a little quiet and we were all more than a little surprised when you started dating him, but... He said he thinks you're a virgin."

Please, if there is a God, open this damn floor and pull me through it...

"No, that's not what he said," Courtney, the only one to not have a comment yet, finally speaks. Just how many of my so-called friends has he been talking to behind my back? "He said that you were a cock tease."

That *asshole*.

I get that maybe I'm a little "old-fashioned" and don't enjoy the hook-up culture.

I like sex.

I like the way it feels, I like the rush, all of it. I just don't need to have it all the time. Yes, I think sex is important in a relationship, but I also think sex can tell you things about your partner...

And I learned with Josh that maybe we weren't going to be compatible. He was...

Selfish in bed.

To put it nicely.

I originally wrote it off as a singular experience. You can't always determine how good someone is in bed after one rushed night that involved alcohol. Now I'm glad I never opted for a second round to double-check.

I swallow hard and fight to retain my composure. "Not that it's anyone's fucking business, but no, I am not." Looking toward Courtney, I say, "A cock tease *or* a virgin. And for *your* information," I swing my glare to Lisa, "he and I *have* slept together. And yes, I told him we needed to slow down. I just prefer to know a guy before I let him stick his cock in me." Now, it's Shaina's turn to be the recipient of my wrath. "And I'd say it's probably a pretty fucking dirty one if he slept with you, so thank the good Lord I stopped before he could give me something. How many notches are you up to now?"

"*Sophia!*" Courtney gasps. "We are not tearing down each other's crowns."

My jaw drops. Is she fucking for real?

They can tear me down, but I'm not allowed to give it back?

Fuck. Them.

Fuck every single one of them.

"Well, I can't help it if he likes my pussy more than he likes to cuddle on a couch with you," Shaina fights back, a stupid fake babying tone to her dig. "I don't know, maybe it was the third time? Fourth? Nah, I actually think it was last night when he told me he has to figure out how to dump poor, pitiful you. All while he pounded his fat cock in me from behind."

"You..." I feel like I'm supposed to cry. Or scream. Or something. But all I have in me is anger. "You are a fucking bitch," I tell her instead, the words coming out far calmer than I'm feeling. "I hope he gives you a disease."

"That was uncalled for, Sophia," Courtney mediates and I give her my middle finger in response.

"Fuck you all."

"Oh, grow up, Sophia!" Jane cuts in. "You think you're better than us, but really? You're stuck in fucking high school."

If anyone is stuck in high school, it's them.

Shaking my head, I push away from the table, forgetting that Em has a hold of my arm. "I'm not doing this. Have a happy fucking birthday."

Em drops my arm but jogs after me, not saying a word until we've pushed free of the bar.

"I'm so sorry, Soph."

Turning on her, I point back to the building. This time, tears fill my eyes and I don't bother blinking them back. "Did you know?"

Her eyes widen at the near accusation as she holds both hands up. "I didn't. I swear. I promise on my Nena's grave."

Considering how much she loved her late grandmother, I believe her.

But before what just happened went down, I thought I could trust every one of those girls with my life. With my secrets.

Apparently not.

"I just want to go home. I don't want to be here," I say, shaking my head.

"I'll walk with you."

Guilt overcomes me. "Are you sure? You were having fun."

"Sophia," Em deadpans. "*You* are my closest friend in that group. Sure, we live together, but even if I lived with one of them, you are still my best friend. Fuck them."

For the first time since the ordeal started, I feel a smile fighting to break free. My best friend does not swear so to hear her say the F-word of all words, has me on the edge of hysterical laughter.

That may actually be the adrenaline letdown happening, but I'll take it either way.

"Okay."

"For what it's worth," she says, throwing an arm around my neck as we retrace our steps from the earlier crawl, "I always thought you were way too good for him."

With a chuckle that's not quite funny, I shake my head.

"You say it as if he and I were dating longer than a few months."

"Soph," she deadpans, her chin lowered and brows up as she regards me with wide eyes, all while we continue walking down the busy sidewalk, "I knew it the very first morning. You were not yourself. Sure, the sex may have been great—"

"It honestly wasn't."

"—but your entire energy changed. He wasn't good for you. He constantly wanted you to go out and never bent when you asked to stay in. He couldn't take a hint when the only time you wanted to do something as a group was when there were only a couple of us. You repeatedly let him make the decisions and didn't speak up for yourself when it was *draining* you."

"Wow," I mumble, "tell me what you really think." I'm not angry with her for laying it out as she saw it, although I do wish she'd said something before it became tonight's episode.

"Let him fuck them. Because you know what? You're too good for them too. You'll find a guy who loves you for you and your cuddle on the couch ways—" there isn't a single ounce of pity in her words, just hardcore encouragement, "and instead of draining you, he'll light you up. You'll find a guy like that because you deserve a guy like that."

"Dang, Em." I lift a hand to wipe away a sudden tear, regardless of the oxymoronic need to chuckle. "Everyone needs a friend like you." Speaking of friends... "I'm sorry I kept them in our lives for so long."

"Eh. It's easy to grow apart from friend groups but sometimes it's hard to see when you're moving in different directions. They're a bunch of bitches, anyway."

I stop in the middle of the sidewalk, not caring in the

least as a group nearly plows into our backs and swears because we stopped, to pull her into a hug. "Thank you for being my friend."

"Of course." She rubs a hand up and down my back as we hug before pulling away. "Now, if we could hustle so we can get back inside, that'd be great. Freaking tanktops in March?"

Laughing, I nod. "I know, right?"

We near the knock-off Irish bar the group stopped at second tonight. Just a few doors down is O'Gallaghers—an Irish pub run by the Irish-American family by the same name—where we started our crawl. Our apartment complex is about a ten minute walk from there but...

"You know, I think I might want to stop at O'Gallaghers again," I tell Emina. They're known to have sports playing on their televisions—there's a hockey game tonight that I chose to miss for this stupid crawl—and it's never a rowdy place. Normally, after being out for nearly two hours and having it culminate in the way it did, I'd kill to go home and curl up in bed right.

Except, I'm not quite ready to sit alone with my thoughts.

"Oh. Um... Okay."

Looking over at my friend, I smile lightly. "You don't have to come in with me."

"No, I'll come in for one. And if you want to stay, I'll just get an Uber or something. I don't know that I want to walk over the bridge alone." She laughs at the last part, but it's one of the "fears" we've both had since moving to our place.

Nothing *bad* has happened on the bridge.

There have just been enough bad things to happen on

other bridges in the country that we both joke we won't cross it solo, especially not when either of us has been drinking.

Unlike when we arrived earlier, O'Gallaghers is busy when we walk in.

Before, we were one of the first groups to enter. Now, every table is taken.

"I see something at the bar." Emina grabs my hand, pulling me through the throng of people. It's a Thursday night at a bar—ladies night. The majority of the crowd is indeed female but to my enjoyment, both televisions flanking the bar have tonight's hockey game on.

I played through the eighth grade but there weren't any good girls' hockey programs in my town for high school aged girls, so I switched to lacrosse.

Lacrosse paid for college and was how I met Megan and Jane.

Now that my thoughts circled back to those girls, my growingly better mood begins to dissipate.

Unfortunately, by the time we make it up to the bar, someone takes the only seat there is. "We can stand," Emina says, shaking her head. "I'm okay with it. Are you?"

Nodding, I look up toward a television. "Yeah. I'm good." The Enforcers are playing Seattle and are up, three to one. There's an entire twenty-minute period for Seattle to come back, but this group of Enforcers has been on fire all season.

I'm not paying much attention to what's going on at the bar because San Diego is on a penalty kill. There's something about a team being a man down that keeps me glued to play-by-play action.

"Hey, ladies, can I get you something?" a smooth voice

cuts through. When I look over, I see our male bartender from earlier leaning into the bar top. The person on the stool in front of us leans out of the way.

"A vodka Sprite, please," Emina answers.

"You?" he asks, looking in my direction.

"I'll do the same." It's not my usual go-to but it's easier to just get what Em's getting as the noise of the pub grows louder and it's harder to hear.

He nods and turns away, and I can't help but admire the way the white shirt he wears stretches over his back. He has visible muscles but isn't the big, body builder type.

And the way his shirt tapers down to his hips...

I immediately imagine what he may look like without a shirt on.

He probably has dimples above his ass.

And he definitely has that well-sculpted V in the front that women go ga-ga over.

Shaking my head at my wayward thoughts, I look back to the television just as the Enforcers' penalty kill team—Porter Prescott, Nico D'Amaco, Rhys Kittner, and Mikey Leeds—slam into a four-man huddle. The scroll at the bottom of the screen announces a short-hand goal.

"Yes," I murmur, catching Emina's attention.

"One man down?"

Nodding, I grin, "Yep."

Emina's family is from Bosnia, although her mom was pregnant with her when they became refugees. They're big soccer fans but Emina will watch hockey with me as long as I watch "football" with her.

"Not bad," she chuckles, looking back to the bar as the bartender comes back. I think he said his name was Jake before. I was still in my working-to-be-a-functioning-social-human frame of mind at that point of the night.

Emina leans in and grabs the first offered drink, handing it back to me, before taking the second. "Thank you," we say at the same time, and he grins, a quick nod of his head.

"Sure thing. You ladies opening a tab?"

My friend looks at me, probably because she's only interested in staying for one drink. Shrugging as I nod, I lean in. "Yes. Please."

"Sophia?" he asks, probably to assign a name to it.

I try not to take it to heart—bartenders know their patrons—but after the night I've had, him remembering my name from an hour before sends a warm thrill through me. "Yeah. Sophia. Do you need my card?" I turn my phone over to slide my debit card free, but Jake waves me off as he grins crookedly.

"You're good. I trust you. Just let me know if you ladies need anything else."

"Gosh, he's beautiful," Emina mumbles after he walks away.

I have to agree, and I'm not at all jealous to realize we both find the bartender attractive, considering the way my night's gone.

It's one thing to appreciate the same type of man as your friend, but another thing entirely to sleep with your friend's boyfriend.

Besides, it's not like either of us are extroverted enough to act on the attraction.

How do you pick guys up at a bar? I have zero clue. My "is he flirting?" meter broke in high school.

I'd met Josh after a month of swiping left and right—which should have been my first clue—and before him, I dated a guy in college I met during an athletics meeting.

Emina and I stand and watch the hockey game, sipping on our drinks. When the seat in front of us becomes vacant,

Em pushes me forward. "Sit! I'm going to head out soon, anyway." I take the stool but turn my back to the bar so I can face and talk with my friend.

Soon though, she's ordering a ride on her phone and before I know it, I'm alone.

Turning to face the pine, I place both of our glasses down and push them closer to the other edge. Satisfied, I prop my cheek in my hand and focus on the closest television. The period is just about over and I'm wondering what the heck I'm going to do with myself during the eighteen minutes between the second and third periods. It's not like I can hear the announcer's commentary that will happen between periods. Maybe I can play on my phone...

"Where'd your friend go?" Jake's smooth voice interrupts my thoughts.

I drop my hand to my forearm that's laying on the bar top and tip my head in the direction of the door. "She had to go."

"Do you need to close out?" He looks remorseful. "I didn't notice you guys were done, I'm sorry."

"No, I'm staying for a bit." I wave him off, before adding, "It's okay."

"All right. Can I get you something else to drink?" Jake stacks our two used glasses after dropping the straws into what I can only assume is a garbage of some sort.

"What flavored vodkas do you have?" Because I've been on the liquor train, I may as well stay on it. At least with vodka, I can nurse them until I'm ready to face the silence of being home.

"The usual fruity flavors, but if you're looking to be a little more adventurous, we just got in Effen Blood Orange. Could pair it with your Sprite again, or a seltzer, if you'd rather get the full taste of the orange."

"Sure." I nod. "Let's do it. Speltzer," I blush at the combination of drinks. "Seltzer. Sorry. I swear I'm not drunk. I just...mash my words, sometimes."

Thankfully, he laughs. "I've done it too. I'll be right back."

He walks away to go to the center of the bar, where they have a wall of liquor, pulling down a glass bottle with an orange colored label. Instead of mixing it down there, he brings the bottle back to where I sit.

After nodding toward my hand, his attention turns to pouring vodka into a glass. "You didn't get too far tonight."

I look down to where he gave his pointed look and notice the colorful marks on my hand. O'Gallaghers didn't have hand stamps tonight but there's a red circle with a smiley face from bar two, and a neon green X that was done with marker from the third place. "Everyone decided that twenty-five wasn't so fun to celebrate and ended the night early?" he jokes, glancing up through his long, dark eyelashes.

Gosh, it's not fair that men get the great eyelashes.

"No. They're still out there, I'm sure." I watch as he pulls the soda hose out. It's a little too loud to hear the pop and fizz as he fills the glass but I can imagine it. "We had a bit of a falling out, if you will."

"That's too bad." He sets the mixed drink in front of me. "Let me know if you need anything else, okay? Do you want a menu?"

"No, thank you," I answer, although I should probably start consuming carbs if I hope to make it out of the night in one piece. I may not drink a lot but I know that carbs will allow me to drink longer. "I'll be okay for now, but thank you."

"Not a problem."

I force myself to look back at the game, and not watch him walk away.

THREE

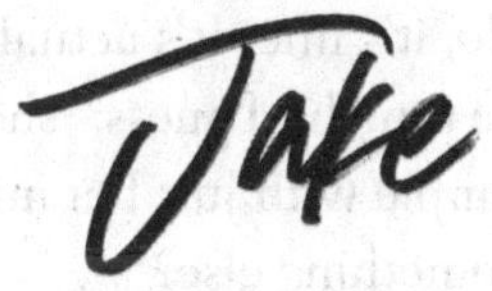

I LEAVE Sophia to her drink and work with a couple other patrons, some closing out, others just starting their night. Regardless of how busy it is, my mind keeps circling back to her at the end of the bar.

When she and only one of her six friends came back, I was shocked. I kept waiting for the rest of the group to come back after seeing the first two, but it was quickly apparent the others weren't joining.

Glancing at the clock, I see it's nearing eight. Thirty minutes ago I was hoping Conor would come in sooner than later but now that Sophia's back, I'm okay with him taking more time. Not that I'm the guy who hits on a patron but there's something about the woman's demeanor that continues to snag my attention. Earlier, she was quiet but didn't seem down by any means.

Now, her quietness has an edge of sadness about it.

She's currently sitting alone with her drink hardly

touched, her eyes locked on the television. Looking further over my shoulder, I see the Enforcers are still up but only by one goal.

When the couple sitting next to her leaves, I take the excuse to move back to her end of the bar and start up a conversation. Clearing the glasses, I point to hers. "Not good?"

Glancing from her hardly touched drink to me, she shakes her head. "No, it's fine. It's actually really good. I'm just...somewhere else tonight, I guess," she adds with a small smile, tapping her temple with just her middle finger.

"Can I get you something else?"

"No. Really." Her smile widens. "This is great. Thank you."

I finish my current tasks and push into the back of house to drop food plates in the industrial sink, running into Saint returning from his thirty-minute break.

"You're still here?" he asks, hanging his zipper-hoodie on a row of hooks. "I thought Conor was coming in."

"He said it could be eight before he got here, but it could be nine that he finally rolls in and I'd be okay. I'm not here tomorrow."

We both walk into the busy pub and he chuckles behind me. "It's because Bachelorette Number Seven came back," he observes.

"It was a birthday party," I remind him.

"Yet he doesn't deny the statement."

I don't hesitate to flip him off while grinning, but my smile quickly falls as I consider the woman who has my attention. "She looks fucking sad, doesn't she?"

Sophia's watching the game again and doesn't seem to notice that we're both looking in her direction.

"She's drinking wrong, then." He steps away and

toward the digital jukebox. As the Dua Lipa song comes to a close, the dance-pop morphs into an upbeat country song.

"Ey? Ey?!" Saint points upward to a speaker as he comes back, a shit-eating grin across his face. The words start to come through, and I recognize it as *Drinkin' It Wrong* by Adam Doleac.

"It's a good song," I concur with an amused grin, "but she's pretty caught up in the game."

One of my other patrons raises a finger so we split up, Saint for the floor and me for my customer. I get him another beer and when he's settled, I move back to Sophia.

"Seriously, I can get you something else," I tell her, reaching for the mostly untouched drink. "I mean, I know we have a fun atmosphere, but if you're trying to get your mind off something, not touching your drink isn't the way to go about it."

For the first time since meeting her, she smiles a full smile at me. I thought she was pretty before, but now I'm struck by how very attractive I find her. "I was just listening to the lyrics of the song that's playing. It's pretty fun. But no. Honestly. This is fine." She pulls the glass back toward her before lifting it up to her plush pink lips, holding the straw back with her index finger and drinking straight from the glass. Swallowing, she nods as she puts it down. "This is actually really good vodka. It's smooth... I like it. You said it was Effen Blood Orange?"

Needing something to do with my hands, I pull the bar towel from where it hangs out of my back pocket and dry a spot on the bar beside her. "It is. It's named from a Dutch term that means smooth and even, so I guess they did it right."

"It's fitting for my night. The 'effen' part. Well, not the fact it's a Dutch term but, you know, like...slang.

31

Would that be right? Slang? Whatever. You get what I mean."

I chuckle, even as I have a feeling her rough night has something to do with why only she and one friend came back, versus the whole group. And while bartenders are cheap therapists, I'm not one to pry someone's bad day from them.

If a person wants to unload, great. But I won't force it.

Especially with a woman like Sophia.

Earlier when she was with the group, I was drawn to her quiet nature. She stood out among her loud friends. Now, that draw remains but I've had time to take in more of her beauty.

She still wears the black tank top from earlier, and her light hair is straight, flowing down and around her shoulders. I'd probably call it blonde, but maybe it's light brown. It's thick though, I can tell just by looking.

Beyond her looks, is the way her eyes seem to take everything in. The game on the television. The friends that are laughing down at the other end of the bar. The way our staff moves in and out of the back, the door swinging with each person.

The longer I study the woman, the more I want to ask why she seems sad, and again...

Not my place to pry.

"Well, if you need a refill, let me know. I'm probably heading out soon, but by no means do you have to close out. I'll just pass you over to one of the others."

"Thank you, Jake."

"You're welcome, Sophia."

Except, Conor still doesn't come in at eight, and after I got Sophia to start her drink, she finishes it quickly. I line a second one up for her, but comp it on her tab. This one gets drained far faster than the first, and when she waves me down, I'm prepared to get her a third but she stops me before I can.

"Can I switch to beer?"

"You absolutely can." The beers on tap are usually going to be cheaper than our liquors, and the Effen Blood Orange is a little pricier than one like Smirnoff.

"What would you suggest?" She leans into the bar, her arms crossed on top, supporting her.

"Well, the bosses started their own brew a year or so ago. It's pretty good. It's an Irish beer, so it's fairly stout but it's not as dark as, say, Guinness. We don't usually have it year-round but we're prepping for St. Patrick's Day."

"Sold. I'll try it."

I pour her one from the tap, tipping the glass until it's just over halfway filled before leveling it off to give just under an inch of head. Satisfied, I bring the beer to the light-haired beauty, placing it in front of her.

"Go ahead and give it a taste. If you don't like it, I can get you something more commercial."

She takes a sip, nodding as she brings the glass back down and wiping the back of her hand over her mouth. "Mm. That's good. The caramel and toffee are strong, but it's a good strong."

"I'll be sure to pass that along," I chuckle, leaving her to her game and beer. Now that it's after eight, the post-dinner crowd is coming in. While most of the afternoon and early evening ebbs and flows, there won't be any slowing down now. Not until after midnight.

I'm busy on the other side of the bar when Sophia calls for a refill, but it's Shayne who gets her set up. Just like her second vodka drink, this second beer goes down quickly. I watch as she starts a conversation with the woman next to her, although it's short-lived because someone's at the jukebox and it's becoming a party in here. While in her seat, Sophia starts to rock back and forth, her shoulders swaying with the beat. She mouths the words to the song—well, I assume she mouths them; she may very well be singing—as her eyes remain glued to the television, watching the final minutes of the Enforcers game.

"I am so fucking sorry," Conor's big voice booms behind me as he pushes through the swinging door separating the back from front. "Just as Aiden and I finished up dinner and he was getting ready to go to a friend's, he starts puking all over. I don't know how the hell he got a stomach bug while everyone else has the flu, but shit, it's a mess at my house."

The man looks tired, but if there's one thing Conor O'Gallagher is, it's a great owner and manager. I don't know Rory much, he doesn't come into San Diego all that often, but between Brenna and Conor, they keep the place running at a high level. Brenna and her husband, Stone, are big fixtures here, but Conor lives and breathes two things—his family and O'Gallaghers.

"It's not a problem. You forget you've been on your feet all day once the next wave comes in," I joke, although I'm serious. "Shayne hasn't had a break yet. I'm happy to stay longer." I glance in Sophia's direction. I can't deny that I'm feeling some sort of way about her, and staying to make sure she's okay is part of the reason I offer.

Besides, I have nothing to do tomorrow. What's another thirty minutes at work?

"Are you sure? I can handle it without you if you're dead."

"I'm good."

Shayne heads to her break right when Conor points in her direction, and while she's supposed to take thirty, I wouldn't be surprised if she's back in twenty. When Sophia waves me down again, I'm assuming she's ready to close out.

"You done for the night?" I ask, reaching for her empty glass.

"Nope. I'm just finally starting to feel really good, ya know?"

I have a moment of "responsibility" panic, as I realize she's probably had one too many. But she seemed absolutely fine before! Did that second beer really hit her that hard?

"How about a water? How you getting home?" I ask in a far calmer tone than I'm feeling, pouring water from the hose without her agreeing to it.

"I'm not drunk," Sophia mumbles, although she does reach for the glass and takes a large gulp.

"I...didn't say that you were. But you also haven't eaten." Fuck me, I should have offered her a menu more than the one time.

She waves me off. "Nah. I'm fine. Honest."

While I don't believe that she's *not* drunk, I certainly won't be serving her any more tonight. If she doesn't leave before I do, I'll be sure to pass that along.

I'm also going to slide her basket of mini tacos and make up some excuse about them being made by accident.

"You didn't answer my other question though. Do you have a ride home?"

"I walked. Well, we all walked. Together. As a group. Did you know one of my best friends slept with my boyfriend?" She puts the water glass down and *pffts*. "She had the odd...odd..." she frowns momentarily as the word seems stuck on her tongue, "aud*acity* to say it was because I didn't put out, and he needed to fuck someone, so she was ever so helpful to do that for him."

And just like that, the vault of "Why Sophia's Down" opens.

I keep what I'm feeling tamped down, but I'm having a hard time figuring out why someone would have Sophia, yet *cheat* on her. Cheating is a coward's game if you ask me, but if I had a woman like the one sitting on the other side of the bar, I'd do everything in my power to keep her.

Not run her off.

"Is that why you and your one friend came here alone? Not with the group?"

"Ding, ding, ding. You're smart, Jake. But you probably hear sob stories all the time, don't you? You're really pretty, did you know that?" She melts into her folded arms at the change of subject. The resemblance to the Babs Bunny "heart eyes" GIF my sister, Hollis, likes to use has me grinning.

"Can I call someone to walk home with you?" I ask instead of having Sophia elaborate. "Or I can get you an Uber." I'm not entirely pro-rideshares, thanks to an event my other sister, Chandler, went through in high school. I just...don't trust people to an extent, I guess.

"I don't like to be in cars with strangers."

"That's probably smart. What about your friend?"

"Shaina? The one who slept with Josh?" she spits out and I have to fight to not chuckle at the distaste on her face.

"No. The one you came back with." I'm glad she hasn't called me out on only remembering her name.

"Oh. Em. Emina. No, she's probably sleeping already. Her bedtime's seven, usually. And here everyone was giving me a shit time for not wanting to go out. Em's the one who goes to bed early! I just don't like to be out in the hustle and bustle of party central. We're not twenty-one anymore."

Twenty-four, or thereabouts, isn't that far off either, but I let her have her moment.

"You know, college life is different than adult life. I have a *job* I have to worry about. I get to set my own hours though, so that's fun." Her tone travels up and down depending on the words. I've met many people who are animated with their hands but Sophia is animated with her voice. "And I don't have anything to do tomorrow, which was why I was okay going out on a weekday night. But I should probably go to bed soon. It was very, very, *very* nice to meet you, Jake." Then she frowns, tipping her head to the side. "Can I touch your hair? It looks so wavy and soft on top, but you have it shaved on the sides. I bet that feels nice."

"How far away do you live, Sophia?" I find myself asking, the need to know she gets home safely, strong.

Her eyes, which seemed to start crossing—unfocusing, maybe—pop back to mine. "Huh?"

"Where do you live? I don't feel great letting you walk home alone," I'm honest with her. "I'm almost done. I can take you where you need to go."

She squints at me. "You know this bar used to have a reputation."

"Pub." Leaning close, I lower my voice, "Don't call the establishment a bar when Conor is in earshot." It's a bit of a joke, but the O'Gallaghers are very adamant about what the public calls this place, and that is *not* a "bar."

"Sorry. *Pub.*" She enunciates the word all while leaning in closer. The space between our faces is small and fuck, the desire to kiss her hits strong. I could easily close the gap and take her lips with mine. This close, I can make out gold specks in the multitude of shades that make her eyes hazel. She also has light freckles that cover the bridge of her nose.

Are they faded because she covers them up? Or are they fading with age?

Her swallow is practically audible before she pushes back. Does she feel the crazy chemistry, too?

"Anyway. It had a reputation."

I know what she's referring to. Before they were married to their wives, the O'Gallagher brothers weren't quiet about their after-closing endeavors. "That was a long time ago," I clarify, bracing my hands on the pine and stretching my shoulders back.

"So, you're not going to walk me home and have your filthy way with me?"

I should have expected it, but I find myself nearly choking on my spit. While composing myself, I refill her water. "Just sit here and drink this."

"I'm not drunk."

"Okay, Sophia." I grin, pushing the glass closer to her. "Just...don't go anywhere."

FOUR

THE WATER they serve here is *really* good. It's super crisp and refreshing. It goes pretty well with the mini tacos that suddenly appeared in front of me. When I frowned and tried to push them back because as good as they smell, I didn't order them, the other bartender dude—the owner, I think, maybe?—said they were mine and taken care of.

That was good because I would have been sad about saying 'no' to them.

They smelled *really* good.

And tasted even better.

I'd have longingly watched whatever other patron they went to.

I'm pondering my glass—it's empty now but there's a drop of condensation that refuses to fall down the smooth surface—when there's a tap on my shoulder. Startled, I jump and turn on the stool, only to find Bartender Jake on my side of the bar.

"How did you get over on this side so quickly?" I ask him, and his face splits into that crooked smile he's been shooting my way all night.

He probably gives it to all the ladies but I guess I didn't really notice much tonight to tell you if that's the truth or not.

"It's been thirty minutes, Soph. I'm going to get you home, okay?"

"I only live a block away," I tell him while sliding off the stool. "Oh, you're tall." I tip my head all the way back. "I can see up your nose." Something tells me I'm going to regret saying that but I seemingly have zero filter at the moment.

Jake coughs and shakes his head before draping something over my shoulders. "Stuff your arms in there. It's cold." I do as he asks, reveling in the warm sweatshirt fabric. It smells like a man.

"Is it yours?"

He nods.

"Won't you be cold?"

"I'll be fine. You're the one dressed for summer."

"I told Megan it was too cold for freaking tank tops. Tank tops in March at night? So dumb," I say, shaking my head as I try to zip up the sweatshirt. Suddenly, Jake's larger hands are there, and he tugs the pull up.

"I can drive you, or I can walk with you. But I'm going to make sure you get home all right, okay?"

"I don't like to get into cars with strangers."

"You mentioned that."

"Did I? I forgot. I probably shouldn't leave with a stranger, either."

He grins at me again, then points to the corners of the

room. "Cameras. Besides, A, you know where I work, and B, everyone here knows you're leaving with me. I promise you're safe."

"Me thinks all the unsafe people say that to their unnoticing victims."

The upturn of his lips falters slightly and I wonder what I said to make him react that way. Instead, I sigh loudly. "Ugh. Fine. You drive a hard bargain."

He chuckles and I'm not sure if it's at me or if I made a funny joke, but I'm getting tired and know I have to get to bed sooner than later. I definitely overindulged tonight, made worse by heightened emotions and an empty stomach.

Jake yells out "bye" to the bar—excuse me, *pub*—and helps me toward the doorway. There's a series of three steps right out the door, which was probably a bad design decision, if you ask me. With his hand on my elbow, Jake helps me down the stairs safely but once on the flat sidewalk, keeps his hands to himself again.

I wish he wouldn't.

He has very nice hands.

"You said you live a block away? Which direction?"

"That way," I say, jutting my chin up instead of pointing, while stuffing my hands in the pockets of his sweatshirt. It's warm and smells nice.

"Over the bridge?"

"Yeah. The bridge."

"Hm."

"Hm?" I start to ask what he's judging, because he's definitely being a Judgey McJudgerson with that tone, when I suddenly remember all the drinks I consumed. I stop immediately and gasp. Or maybe I gasped and then stopped.

Regardless, he's a step ahead of me and turns, a wrinkle between his brows. Instead of being two or three frown lines going up and down between the thick splices of hair above his eyeballs, he just has one super prominent one. I want to touch it.

"What's up?"

I open my mouth, close it, and then it's my turn to frown. What was it that had my attention? Because right now, all I can focus on is that frown line.

"You need something?" asks Jake the Barten—

"Oh! Yes! Jake the Bartender," I mumble the adjec-verb-tive, whatever, more to myself than aloud because maybe if I *say* "bartender" so I can *hear* it, I won't forget what came to mind.

"Yes, Sophia?" His frown line is gone and now, his brows are raised. The emotion on his face went from concerned to humored, just like that. *Snap*, I think, the fingers of my right hand brushing lightly together in the sweatshirt pocket.

Whispering, I lean closer to him, darting my eyes back and forth to make sure no one can overhear. "I didn't pay my tab."

He chuckles and reaches for my elbow, pulling me along to continue walking. "I covered it. Don't worry."

I take a few quick, short steps before continuing at a normal gait beside him. "But... No, Jake."

"But, yes, Sophia. Don't worry about it. It's done." Again, he drops my elbow and I huff out a breath at the loss.

We walk beside one another in silence, the road noise and nightlife our soundtrack. The bridge has a lip on the pathway that I usually remember...

But do not tonight.

"Shit." Jake reaches out to catch me before I can land on

my face—because I didn't have the wherewithal to remember to take my hands out of the sweatshirt pockets. "You okay?" He pulls me back to stand tall, moving my body so I'm standing in front of him.

Gosh, he's even prettier up close.

It's dark, but I think his eyes are light brown. Like the amber glass bottles that so many people were tipping back tonight. His nose has a slightly flat ridge as if he'd been hit in the nose at least once.

Tipping my head, I can't stop myself from asking about it. "Did you break your nose?"

He lifts a hand and touches the flattened part. "I did. When I was nineteen. Are you okay?"

"Oh. Yeah. You did ask that, didn't you? I'm fine," I smile up at him. I'm starting to understand why people like to get a little past tipsy.

You feel like you're floating.

You don't have a single care in the world.

And I needed that tonight.

To not have a single care.

Because after hearing about Josh...

"You know... I hate your species," I blurt out. "No, hate's a strong word. I dis*like*. No. Nope, hate's definitely the better word," I correct, starting to move off the bridge—but apparently back in the direction we came from.

Jake's hand hooks in my elbow, turning me around. "This way, Soph."

"Oh. Yeah. Okay. My place." I change direction, cautiously stepping back onto the bridge and avoiding the lip that caught me last time. "Are you coming to my place too?"

He keeps his hand loosely hooked, guiding me over the bridge as if I can't be trusted to do it on my own. Then again, I think I just proved I'm a walking hazard right now. "Just walking you home."

The bridge isn't a long one, maybe ten feet...thirty feet...okay, I don't really know. But we're in the middle before Jake says, "We're not all bad."

I stumble over my feet again. "Well, shit, my toes don't work tonight. Who's not all bad?"

"Men."

Once I'm steady on my feet, Jake drops my elbow but doesn't keep his hands away for long. I feel the heat of his palm on my lower back, although he's not pushy about the touch. "Not all men are bad. I'm sorry you got a shitty one."

"Not the first, won't be the last."

"You should probably work on your selection skills, then."

"You can't tell me that you, a man, don't want to fuck, fuck, fuck everything."

His fingertips press lightly against the sweatshirt material, but only for a moment. "A real man isn't going to date one woman and sleep with another behind her back."

If only all men thought that way. "You talk a good talk, Jake the Bartender." At the other end of the bridge, I slow down, focusing on where I know the lip to be...and still nearly take a spill onto the concrete.

"Good lord, woman," Jake mutters, once again taking my elbow. "You're going to end up in the water."

"Well, it's a good thing you're with me then, isn't it?"

His answer is practically a growl, and I wonder for a second what that's about. In the next second though, I'm thinking about that growl being in my ear, while we're in bed and his cock... "I live over that way," I choke out. "The townhouse apartments." How those words came out instead of word vomiting what his growl does to me, I have no idea. Guess I have some self-control, after all.

It doesn't take us long to walk onto the complex property, and it's a good thing too because I'm suddenly very, very sleepy. "I'm in the back corner. Building 35," I say around a yawn, not registering the fact he unlocks the pedestrian gate with a fob on his keys. "You don't have to walk me there." Surely the man has other things he'd rather be doing on a Thursday night.

"I'm not taking you halfway and then leaving you to fend for yourself in this maze."

I've never thought of it that way but yes, the complex is a bit maze-like. "Don't complain to me then—" I yawn again, this time, speaking while my mouth is stretched wide — "if you miss out on whatever it was you were going to do after work."

"Had no plans."

We continue walking and it's almost like he knows where he's going, which should concern me. If I were level-headed, it would *definitely* concern me...

"So close," I mumble, "yet so, so, so far away..."

Jake chuckles beside me. "What unit are you?"

I tell him and soon it's in sight. You know those times when you're sleepy in the car and you get a sudden burst of energy the nearer you get to your destination?

That's not what happens to me tonight.

If anything, I get ten times sleepier knowing my bed is just a few yards away.

The apartment complex is set up in a series of four-unit, two and three-story townhomes, each with a small iron gate by the front stoop. Most of the units have a front door that opens to a small foyer and staircase, with the main floor being the second level thanks to an attached two-car garage.

The corner units have L-shaped patios, with their front doors on the side of the building, but I have a middle unit with a small concrete slab as a "porch." The middle units have a five-by-four section of grass that the amenities list calls a yard, and the moment Jake opens the gate inward, I find the wooden Adirondack chair Emina bought a few weeks ago, plopping down hard immediately.

"Hey, now. You're practically inside. C'mon. Back up." He tugs on my arm but I'm just too tired to care.

"Just leave me here," I mumble, tipping my head back to rest on the wood. "I can sleep here."

"Nope. Not happening. Let's go, Soph."

I can feel the energy draining from my body. It's hard to keep my eyes open so I give in to the need to close them.

"Soph. Sophia. C'mon." He's tugging on my arm again and I whimper in complaint. It's officially a no bones day for me.

No bones night.

No bones moment.

Whatever.

It's boneless.

And now I think I maybe want to cry because the Bones or No Bones Day dog *died*.

But I don't cry.

I don't even open my eyes when suddenly I'm swooped into a cradle hold. My relaxed body simply leans more fully into the hold, my head on Jake's shoulder. I nuzzle in closer, and my nose gets a whiff of him.

He smells like a man.

Like the sweatshirt I wear, but more powerful.

More potent, is the right *P* word.

He smells really, really good.

"Yous'ellgood." It's official. My lips no longer work.

I'm point-two seconds away from being gone for the night.

Jake chuckles as he carries me the few feet to the door.

"I need you to wake up enough to punch the code in, Soph."

"Hmmm...?"

"You have to unlock the door."

Instead of opening my eyes, I mumble the six-digit combination that will unlock the townhouse. I should worry about giving a man who's essentially a stranger the code that grants him access to my home but again...

Too tired to care.

Maybe in the morning Em and I can figure out how to change it.

If I remember.

The next thing I know, I'm in my bedroom and he's lowering me to my bed. I wonder how he knew to take me all the way upstairs? Maybe he accidentally walked into Emina's room. Or maybe I told him and I just don't remember.

"Thank you," I manage to say when my back hits the bed. I feel my shoes being removed and then my covers being tugged as I roll to my side. Soon, I'm cocooned in the heat of blankets.

And just like that...

It's lights out.

THE FIRST THING I realize in the morning is that I hurt. Badly.

My head feels like it's going to pound right off.

The next thing I realize is I'm still dressed, while

wearing a sweatshirt that smells like a cologne I don't recognize.

Squinting my eyes as I force them open, I'm thankful to see I'm in my bed—and in my bed alone. I think back to last night. It's all a bit fuzzy after Jake the Bartender introduced me to the owner's beer.

Like an old movie, snapshots of the following hour or so flash across my mind with a broken record effect on the bridge. Either I stumbled six times, or my brain wants to remind me I made an absolute fool of myself.

"Ugh," I groan, dropping my arm over my eyes. I don't remember everything I said or everything I did, but I do know I was very likely *not* on my best behavior.

All because of fucking Josh and Megan and Shaina.

The thought of them has my head pounding harder and I know I have to do something about it before the ache gets to the point of no return.

Rolling to my side, I gingerly pull my legs out of bed and push to sit at the edge, all while squeezing my eyes shut. This is not fun.

It takes some convincing but eventually, I pry my lids open—and right away, notice the water bottle and piece of paper on my nightstand. I reach for the note, frowning at the unrecognizable, but masculine, scrawl with a phone number at the bottom.

You're probably going to be hurting when you get up but you had a rough few hours. Drink fluids. The O'Gallaghers would suggest you eat a huge breakfast. Avoid Tylenol but go ahead and take ibuprofen.

After that, there's a section that's been scribbled out so much that even if I had the energy to, I wouldn't be able to decipher what's under the mess of lines and circles.

But then the note is signed:

You deserve better friends—M aside.
—Jake "The Bartender"

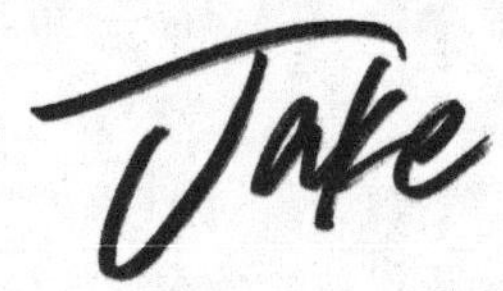

I CLOCK in at four on Saturday, the biggest night of O'Gallaghers' St. Patrick's Day weekend festivities. I'm closing with Ben, Cash, Saint, and Nick tonight, but I wouldn't be shocked if Colie and Shayne stay a few extra hours after their shifts. Conor sent a group text earlier in the day saying he could come in at any point but he'd also texted yesterday to tell everyone he got hit with whatever bug was going through his house—it was the consensus of the group he's better off staying home and far away from the pub.

The last thing we need is to be Ground Zero for a late-season flu outbreak.

We're already busy and likely have been since the parade concluded a few hours earlier. I usually drive to work but because it was so crazy downtown today, I opted to walk.

Walking back over the bridge for the third time in three

days—Thursday night, then on Friday morning to collect my truck, and again today—had me thinking about the hazel-eyed woman who hasn't been too far from my mind in the last thirty-six plus hours.

The one who amazingly lives in the same apartment community as Ben and me.

Except Ben and I live clear on the other side, so even though I've *wondered* why I'd never seen Sophia before Thursday, it's easy to *know* why.

I know my immediate neighbors, and I recognize a few vehicles in different sections of the community, but there are simply too many people to know or recognize everyone.

At the moment, Shayne and I have the bar while the others working are running from bar to floor to back. The O'Gallaghers Original—OG—that I had Sophia try the other night is a hit with the crowd today, and between that and the always popular on St. Patrick's Day in America, "green beer," I've already had to switch out kegs and despite having multiple lines going, I know it won't be the last time today, either.

We have a couple of games going that the pub plays every year for the festivities. First, there's the ridiculous game of "pin the four-leaf clover on the leprechaun's ass," and the leprechaun cut-out is more "Jolly Green Giant" than tiny mischievous thing. The four-leaf clovers, though, are just about real-life sized, so it makes the game—and figuring out the winner for the hour—more interesting. The person who gets the four-leaf clover closest to the marked spot on the leprechaun gets a party-sized platter of cheeseburger shalaylees. It's our most popular appetizer—a wonton-like wrap stuffed with seasoned ground beef and melted American cheese. They're served with Guinness-infused ketchup.

Some might say that's a stupid prize—*give out beer! T-shirts!*

But the people have spoken, and it's the shalaylees they want.

The second game we have going isn't so much a game as a "shame."

If you walk into O'Gallaghers with a shirt saying "Patty," you are required to sing for your supper, so to speak. There have already been ten men—and one woman—who've had to go up on the rarely used karaoke stage and belt out "I'm a little teapot" in the hour I've been here.

There's bound to be many more before the night is through.

However, if you walk in with a shirt proclaiming that it's "Paddy's" day, you get a gold coin that you can use on one alcoholic beverage of choice.

So what about those who don't have Patty or Paddy on their shirt? But they're wearing green, or proudly proclaiming they're Irish, so kiss them?

All St. Patrick's Day-dressed patrons get a wooden coin that they can either keep to redeem for a free drink or appetizer at a later date, or they can write their name and number on the coin before dropping it into one of three raffles we have for the weekend.

They're not "boring" prizes, either.

There's a box suite for up to twenty guests to an April Enforcer's game, food and beverage included, courtesy of the team's Prescott family. There's a set of memberships to the San Diego Zoo—probably because the younger O'Gallagher kids would live there if given the choice. Third, there's a weekend trip, all expenses paid, to wine country.

And the thing is, every one of those buckets will have coins by the end of the weekend. People *want* the prizes.

For the majority of us on staff and working today, it's our first year celebrating St. Patrick's Day, O'Gallaghers Style. The exception being Colie and Saint, who have been here for a couple of years and they prepared us in ways the O'Gallagher siblings couldn't.

That's not saying Conor and Brenna don't know how crazy it gets on the holiday—they're well aware—but they've been part of the pub life their entire lives.

St. Patrick's Day is just another busy day, in their books.

Every time the door opens, the crowd erupts in cheers. Saint is working the entrance right now, handing out coins as appropriate, and the cheers usually have something to do with the attire of the group coming in. With half a grin on my face, I echo the cheers as well, pouring another glass of OG. The room is getting louder but it's not unpleasant—simply a constant chatter.

A loud white noise.

There are cheers and laughter and loud—*off-key*—singing happening to the songs on the jukebox. Colie comes up to give Shayne a break and everything is moving smoothly.

"Colie!" a patron yells, and we both look up. It's one of our regulars, Janet—a woman who's probably in her forties and comes every Thursday with two of her girlfriends. Some nights they drink beer, but most nights they drink wine.

All nights, they shoot darts.

"Isn't this Jaxon?" She points up to the ceiling, her motions clear that she wants Colie to listen closely.

Sure enough, through the vibration of voices, Liam Jaxon's latest country single is playing.

We don't have the music playing on a random playlist so

I wouldn't be surprised if Janet put it on specifically to see if she could get a rise out of Colie.

I watch my friend. The towel she's using to quickly dry a glass slows around the lip, but instead of a negative reaction at hearing her former boyfriend singing an upbeat song about country nights and bright stars, a small smile breaks out on her face.

"Yes," she nods. "It is. He's done really great, hasn't he?"

Before I can check on Janet's reaction, someone is calling me at the other end of the bar and I move to tend to others.

I never met Jaxon, but he and Colie started here at the same time. In fact, they grew up together and moved out to San Diego together. But, as luck would have it, Jaxon was "discovered" by someone in the music industry and left for Nashville.

Why Colie didn't go with, I don't know. No one talks about it. I didn't know the guy, so it's not like I have much to offer in conversation.

Therefore, I don't bring it up.

The hours move quickly and soon both Colie and Shayne are off the floor and Ben is on bar with me. I'll get a break as soon as Cash can switch off with me, but with how busy we've gotten, I may forfeit the thirty and just jump in the back for a quick bite to eat.

The groups of people change over, one set for another, but if you didn't know names and faces, you'd never realize. It's getting closer and closer to the evening rush, and on a *regular* night, the party would only be beginning. I have a feeling that come closing time, we'll still have a pretty full house.

With as many patrons as we've had tonight, I couldn't tell you who's come and who's left. At any random point, you realize that a regular was here and no longer is, but the movement is so quick—and the time is moving so fast—it's easy to lose track of everyone.

So explain to me why then, when the front door opened for over the hundredth time tonight, it felt like the world stopped moving for a fraction of time.

Why it felt like the sounds dimmed, and the lights brightened? .

Why it seemed like Saint moved in slow motion to allow the next guests access?

The moment the two females step inside, the world zooms back to real time and I catch my first glimpse of Sophia in nearly forty-eight hours. It's her and her friend. The roommate.

Both women are wearing Kelly green shirts, although Sophia's is a darker green. The roommate is wearing black cropped leggings with her shirt, and Sophia wears denim shorts, showing off shapely thighs.

Shit. She's gorgeous.

I remind myself that she's just coming off a relationship but it doesn't stop the desire from swirling in my gut.

I then *also* remind myself that I left her my number and she didn't use it.

Maybe she was embarrassed—not that she has anything to be embarrassed about. But I know from having sisters that females think differently than men.

Before I can wave Sophia and her roommate over to the only seat at the bar, Saint is escorting them to the karaoke stage.

Oh no.

I can't stop the wide smile from breaking out on my face, wondering which of the girls broke the Irish St. Patrick's Day "rule." Except, instead of stopping at the stage, he walks them to the prize buckets. From my spot across the bar, I can clearly see he's grinning and chuckling.

Probably flirting.

And for a moment, that pisses me off.

Then I remember I have zero claim to Sophia.

So instead of getting pissy, I force myself to get back to work.

SIX

Sophia

WHEN EMINA CONVINCED me we should head downtown to celebrate St. Patrick's Day—even if only for an hour or two to grab dinner—I wasn't too sure. There would be ample places to celebrate, but the best, hands down, would be O'Gallaghers. And because they would be the best, there was a high likelihood they would be busy.

But it was more than the thought of crowds that had me a touch nervous—cough, embarrassed, cough.

It was the potential of running into Jake.

I spent all of yesterday going over Thursday's events.

Well, after texting Josh and letting him know we were over. The bastard didn't even have the balls to text me back. Whatever.

I digress.

After I texted Josh and called things off, the previous night replayed over and over in my head—and during one of

57

the thousand recaps, I realized I was no longer focusing on the "Megan and Shaina" part, but instead, on the Jake parts.

It certainly hasn't helped that I have his sweatshirt and it's spent the last day mocking me from the corner of my room. I'm going to have to face him to give it back to him at some point. Just...preferably later than sooner.

Like we did on Thursday, Emina and I walk into town. Regardless if we stay out late or not, it's probably safer to walk—we can't control everyone else on the road after a night of celebration.

Once we get to the authentic Irish pub, I'm relieved that our first contact at O'Gallaghers isn't Jake.

"Happy St. Patrick's weekend, ladies," the bouncer-like guy says when we make our way up the three steps to the propped-open door. He has a clean-cut beard that, although dark, is colored green. That's not where his green stops, though. He wears a dark green shirt with the O'Gallaghers barley emblem across his chest. "Nice shirts."

When Emina broke into my room earlier, she threw a green t-shirt at me and told me to put it on. In bold letters, it says "Fuck You" on it, but the F is crossed out with fake Sharpie, an L in its place, and a Y added to the end, effectively changing "Fuck" to "Lucky." There's also a Sharpie-drawn four-leaf clover after "you." I love it.

Emina's shirt is funny too, although I'm glad she's the one wearing it.

Hers proudly proclaims she puts the double-D in "Paddy."

It's a great shirt...but I don't have double-Ds to support it. Although if I did, the top is probably still a little "loud" for my taste.

The door guy asks for our IDs and after we show them, he hands us both a wooden coin and a golden coin. "Gold for not breaking Irish rules. Patty with two Ts is a girl," he chuckles. "You can use it today for one alcoholic drink of your choice. Wooden one is for dressing festive. You can hold onto it for a drink or app at another date, or drop it into one of the prize buckets."

Emina grins. "Oh, prizes? I never win anything. What kind of prizes?" She loves a good prize.

Never wins...but that doesn't stop her from trying.

"Here, let me take you ladies over. Name's Saint. And you both are...?"

"I'm Emina. This is Sophia."

He snaps his thick fingers, his smile wide beneath the dark beard and mustache covering his face. "Ah. Yes. The non-bachelorette party. You're the sad one," he adds, pointing at me.

I open my mouth but nothing comes out. Instead, I grimace and shrug.

"It was a bad night," Emina says for me. "She could use a good prize."

"You were watching the game, right?" Saint asks, walking us across the pub floor, over near a small stage, two dart boards, and three pinball machines.

"I was. I love hockey."

"She's *obsessed*. She used to play."

"Long time ago," I brush off. "I just watch now."

"That's cool," Saint answers. "I don't know a damn thing about it, but I like the guys enough." He coughs and I swear his cheeks maybe even get ruddy, but it's a little dim in here so I could be wrong. "Friends. They come in here a lot and we're all friendly. I very much like women. Anyway. One of the prizes is a box at an Enforcers game. That seems up your alley."

At the table with buckets, he takes the time to tell us

about each prize offering, nevermind they all have small signs on them. It's as if he's purposely spending time with us. He might even be flirting with Emina.

Of our college group, she was always the exotic-like one. She has a soft olive tone to her skin, which makes her tan easily in the summer. Her hair is a rich chestnut color and curly.

So freaking curly.

She wears it short these days and spends hours straightening it, but in college, her hair used to go down to her butt.

When it doesn't matter, she can be loud and flamboyant. But when she cares...that's when she shuts down.

While it's funny watching Saint flirt with her, it's clear to me she's not interested but he'll never catch on.

"Well, if you ladies need anything, we've got Ben and Shayne running the floor, and Colie and Jake on bar." The center of my chest starts to itch as nerves jump in. "Have fun." Saint taps the table twice before returning to his spot at the front door, checking IDs and handing out coins.

I'm having a hard time focusing though. The moment he said Jake's name, my head felt like I was underwater. After I spent most of the last two hours convincing myself he wouldn't be here tonight...

Dumb, dumb, dumb.

Of course, he's here tonight! It's probably their busiest night!

"Oh. Jake," Emina grins, writing her name and phone number on her coin before dropping it in the Enforcers bucket. "He was nice, wasn't he?" She knows he walked me home on Thursday but I don't think she realizes what the thought of him is doing to my head.

For all she knows, he's just a bartender here who was kind enough to make sure I got home safely.

Hell, that's all he is! I scold myself. I shouldn't be embarrassed. He did a nice thing for me on a bad night...and that's all she wrote.

"He was," I manage to agree, putting my head down to write on my coin. While the zoo and trip sound fun—and I do enjoy a good, local wine—the box seats game night is what calls my name. Even if I don't have twenty people to take with me, it would be a fun experience.

"Table or bar?" Em asks as we move away from the prize table. Another group of people comes over, taking our spots. Unlike us, they are *not* escorted by Saint, further cementing that Saint was indeed flirting with Emina.

"Table," I answer, not too quickly, I hope. Thankfully, she doesn't say anything and we find a high top available near a giant cut-out of a leprechaun that's taped to the wall. Unlike the other night when we stood around the table, we both climb into the tall chairs. I put my phone on the surface, face down. It has an ambient display, where the time and temperature will flash on if it catches movement. It's handy when I'm working—I can just move my hand over it as it sits at my desk and the time will display—but it can be distracting at times, too.

It's not long after we sit that a woman comes to the table. I think I remember her from Thursday night, but it's all a little fuzzy. She has short blonde hair in a cute, sassy cut that I'd love to try but know I'd never be able to pull off. There's a single streak of green in it, too, something else I'd be afraid to try.

"Welcome to O'Gallaghers, ladies." She places cocktail napkins in front of us both. "I'm Shayne. Can I get you both something to drink?"

"I'll start with whatever's on tap, please," Emina decides. "I'm not picky."

"Sure. And for you?"

"I'll do the same," I answer out of habit, but then I remember the owner's beer. "Actually, the other night I tried a beer the owners made. I don't remember what it's called." Did Jake give me the name? That part of the night is mostly a blur.

"Yep. OG. I can get you that. Anything to eat?"

Emina and I look at one another, and say at the same time, "Shalaylees." What's better than a bite-sized cheeseburger in a wonton boat?

Nothing.

The answer is nothing.

Grinning, Emina adds, "If you could. Please."

"Sure thing. I'll get that order in for you and your drinks out in a moment."

Shayne walks away and I take a moment to look around, taking in the different people. It's busy but not as busy as I figured it would be. I thought for sure it would be standing room only but there's probably a fire code for that.

I wonder if having Saint at the door is as much for giving out coins and checking IDs, as making sure the establishment stays within patron guidelines the city sets.

"Oh, I forgot to tell you." My friend reaches to the middle of the table, laying her hand flat. "I got an inquiry for a destination wedding. *And!* They'd be open to a videographer."

My brows lift and my smile is quick. "Really? Where to?" Emina started shooting weddings last summer, and she does a damn good job. Her client base grew mostly by word-of-mouth but I helped her build an online presence.

"Bali."

"Oh my gosh. Lucky! When do you know if they'll hire you?"

"Well, I have a meeting with them on Wednesday. They're kind of doing the quick elopement thing and were going to use the resort's photographer but stumbled across my Instagram. Do you think you'd like to come with?"

"I mean...sure. I can come to the meeting."

"No, Soph." Her grin is wide, her brows raised, and I realize I misunderstood her comment. "I think you should be their videographer."

My laugh is uncomfortable, but I'm flattered she thinks I'm good enough. "Emina... I just edit videos." Most of my clients are social media influencers and video vloggers. I have two large families that I edit twenty-minute videos for, and a handful that ask me to put together thirty and sixty-second short spots.

"But you're so good behind the camera, too! Yes, your magic is in the editing process, there's no denying that, but I think you'd be perfect as my right-hand man. Woman."

"I don't..." I shrug a shoulder, although now that the idea has been planted, visions of a beach wedding and all the angles I could catch, run through my mind. "I don't know. Would it be fun? Absolutely. But I don't know that I can ask someone to pay me for filming a wedding. Friend's barbeque? Yeah. Sure. Kid's birthday party? Let's do it. But a wedding? That's a big commitment."

"Think about it, please?"

"Oh. I already am," I chuckle, just as Shayne comes back with our drinks. We thank her and both take sips and when I offer to let Emina taste the OG, she does—and immediately makes a face.

"That's stout."

"It's not as stout as it could be though! I like it."

"You said it was the owner's beer? Like, the O'Gallaghers made it?"

"That's what I was told."

"You know... I wonder what the process looks like, making a beer..."

"It's probably not terribly different from making your plum moonshine." I'm sure they're different but likely both take time and patience.

Emina chuckles. "Rakija." It's pronounced *rah-key-ya*, but I've long let go of trying to get all the Bosnian words correct. I can count to ten and say good night, and that's about it. I'm not having a conversation with Emina in her family's language anytime soon.

"Right. Rakija. Oh, speaking of. Krempita. You were going to write out the recipe for my mom."

"Shoot. Yes." She pulls out her phone. "I'm going to put a reminder in my calendar because I'll keep forgetting." My dad's birthday is coming up and both of my parents fell in love with the Bosnian dessert Emina makes over the holidays.

Krempita is made of homemade custard layered in flaky puff pastry. It's light enough you can easily eat an entire cake on your own without realizing you just devoured the full pan.

It practically melts in your mouth.

"I have a plate of shalaylees," a voice to my left says, and when I look over to the person, the first thing I notice is he's like a skinnier Thor. Not that he's skinny-skinny, but he's also not as broad as Chris Hemsworth.

"Thank you," I say as he puts the platter down between us, and when I look over to Emina, I see she's facing the table...but her eyes keep peeking to the side, toward the man. Literally two seconds ago, she was smiling and laughing, and now she's still as a statue.

"Not a problem. Can I get you ladies anything else?"

He looks from me to Emina, but she's having a hard time looking up at him.

"No, I think we're okay," I speak for us both. "Thank you, though."

"Enjoy."

After he's well out of earshot, I reach out to gently slap the back of Em's hand. "You think he's cute."

"Shh!" She shifts in her seat but there's a blush on her golden cheeks. "Let's not announce things like that. Especially not *loudly*."

"I'll go get his name," I tease as I put my hands on the table, pretending to get ready to chase down the man.

"Sophia! No!"

Laughing, I reach for a shalaylee instead, dipping it in the ketchup-mix. "You thought he was cute though, right?"

Emina grabs an appetizer for herself, sitting straight up and shrugging a shoulder before bringing the wonton-boat toward her mouth. "Maybe I did."

"Girlfriend. You became a statue. You were like a deer in headlights. 'Maybe if I sit still, I won't be noticed.' Which is super silly, not wanting to be noticed when you're freaking gorgeous." The words may come out lighthearted, but I mean them.

"Yeah, well..." She doesn't complete the thought.

"'Yeah, well...' You have nothing to add?" I joke, and thankfully, she laughs back.

Grinning, she shakes her head. "Just eat your damn shalaylee and be quiet."

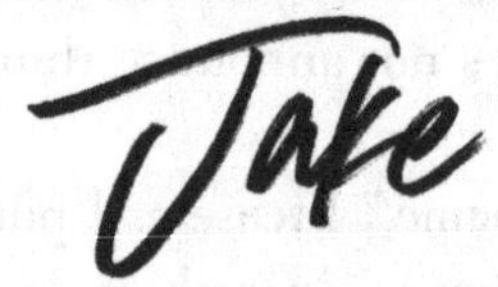

"TAKE YOUR THIRTY, WESLEY," Saint tells me, walking behind the bar. Cash took over at the door and Saint is now in the supervisor role. In the time since Sophia and her friend arrived, I've cooled off my annoyance toward Saint but that hasn't stopped me from glancing across the room in the girls' direction.

Unfortunately, Sophia sits with her back to me, but watching the friend, it seems like they're having a good time.

"Sure thing." O'Gallaghers isn't calm by any means, but it's been tolerably steady. It's probably best if we try and get as many lunch breaks out of the way before the later crowd arrives.

"There's a shit ton of pizza in the office," he adds, moving away from me and toward a patron. "Eat up."

As I'm about to push into the kitchen area, I glance once more in Sophia's direction—at the same time that she turns her head to look over her shoulder. Our gazes collide and hold...yet I don't stop my forward motion, continuing to walk through the swinging door and back toward the office.

I don't make it to the office—and damn, the pizza smells good—before giving in to the desire coursing through me.

I have to see her.

And not just random glances over to her back.

I'm not sure what it is about her that has me hooked. Maybe it was her quiet nature within her group of friends. Or, maybe it was how she slowly came out of her shell the other night. Whatever it was, she's not been far from my mind.

If I get to her table and she's talking, or doesn't seem interested, or hell...if she and her friend have left, I'll just use the excuse I needed to use the restroom.

Happy with my plan, I head back to the busy pub, walking along the back wall, all while my eyes scan the area in front of me until I find her where she'd been for the last near-hour.

Except once again, she's alone.

"Hey, Sophia," I say, with far more confidence in my tone than I'm feeling. She turns her head toward me as I close the distance, crossing my arms on the high-top table. "How's it going?"

With a small smile, Sophia reaches up to push her light hair behind her ear. "Jake. Hi. I wasn't... I didn't..." When she can't finish the sentence, she bites her lower lip. Something about her white teeth pushing into her plump lower lip has blood racing south.

Clearing my throat, I give her a crooked grin. "Your friend... Is it your roommate who's with you tonight? I thought I saw you come in with someone."

Way to play it cool, man.

"Yeah. Emina. She just ran to the restroom."

"Ah. That's what I was about to do but saw you here alone. Just wanted to stop by, see how you were doing. Are you guys enjoying yourselves?"

"We are." She nods a couple of times, her eyes never leaving mine. "I wasn't sure I wanted to come out tonight but Emina loves all the holidays," she says with a small giggle. "I thought O'Gallaghers was going to be the best place for St. Patrick's Day."

"There are a lot of good spots, but I agree. We're probably the best." It's not cocky when it's true.

We smile at one another but before I can ask her anything else, Emina returns.

"Emina, this is Jake."

"Ah, yes. Jake the Bartender," Emina grins, holding out her hand. I shake it, even though we more or less met already. "Thank you for making sure she got home okay the other night."

"It wasn't a problem. I actually live near you guys, so it wasn't a big deal at all."

"Oh?" This came from Sophia.

Nodding, I look back at her. "Yeah. Ben and I—he's been running the floor tonight. The man bun guy—we're over in the first phase, building three."

"The Thor guy," Sophia describes, and I watch her look at Emina with a silly grin. Do they have a thing for Ben?

But it's Emina who blushes, and I think maybe it's just her who might be interested in my roommate.

"He's single," I add, helpfully.

Even through blushing, Emina looks me straight in the eye. "Are you?"

I hear a thump before the brunette gasps, her eyes shooting from me to Sophia.

Chuckling, I nod. "I am." I glance toward Sophia, just through the sides of my eyes, before looking back at her friend. "Not always easy to find the right person in a city like this, you know?"

"Gosh, do we know," she answers, with a roll of her eyes. "The men here can be pigs." Emina reaches out and puts her hand on my forearm, but I don't take it sexually. "I'm sure you're different," she teases, although *I'm* sure there's a level of distrust there, too.

"Not to toot my own horn," I start, looking at Emina, but then turning my attention to Sophia, "I am. We're not all bastards." I don't know how much Sophia remembers from Thursday night but I stand by my word on that subject. "Well, ladies. It was good seeing you both again. I'm going to hit the head and then stuff my face with food before I'm needed back on the floor. Have fun tonight. But be safe."

"We will, Jake the Bartender," Emina grins, at the same time Sophia replies, "Thank you. We will."

I don't *have* to go to the bathroom but I have the break, may as well use it. I take a piss, wash my hands, and head back, telling myself the entire time that I *will not look in Sophia's direction*, even though I literally have to walk next to her table to get back to the front.

But I can't help myself.

Once again, when I look toward her, she looks up and locks eyes with mine.

Going for it, I grin at her and give her a wink as I head to the front and then back to the office.

I'm indeed stuffing my face with a third slice of pizza when my phone goes off in my hand. I've been playing a numbers game called Join Blocks. It's a pretty stupid game but it keeps me entertained when in the quiet office, away from the hustle of the pub.

Looking at the notification, I notice it's a text from an unknown number. Frowning, I open it fully.

UNKNOWN NUMBER:

What time do you work until?

I'm debating whether or not I should answer or mark it as spam when a second text comes through.

UNKNOWN NUMBER:

-Soph

I toss the rest of the uneaten slice on a paper plate in front of me, wiping my hand hurriedly on my jeans, and text her back.

ME:

Close tonight.

After hitting enter, I type out another message.

ME:

I have off Monday though if you want to do something

The message goes from sending, to delivered, to read. I wait a moment to see if she'll text back right away, and sure enough, three dots pop up and start to dance as she begins a reply.

Unfortunately, the dots go away and don't come back.

Sighing, I put my phone to sleep, finish my pizza, and head back to work.

THE NIGHT HAS BEEN crazy yet fun. That doesn't take away from the fact I'm ready for two to hit, though.

The kitchen may have closed at ten, but there are hours of fun to be had...

He thought sarcastically, I think, pouring another round of Guinness for a high top of four guys. "Four up," I say, placing the glasses on a tray. Ben and Saint are on the floor while I mostly man the bar by myself. Cash is doing a bit of both, wherever he's needed most at any given time. We'll have the four of us until midnight when Ben gets to head home. Cash will be the next to leave at one, and Saint and I will close up together an hour later.

I turn from the waiting beers, walking over to help one of my parties of three at the other end. Once they're settled, I go to the register to close out a tab but have to wait for Cash to finish.

After typing onto the flat screen, the cash drawer pops open and Cash removes a few bills, dropping them into the communal tip jar at the same time he pushes the drawer closed.

"She's all yours," he says. As he steps away, I notice a napkin that I'm guessing he put down. I'm about to crumple and toss it as I close out my own tab but there's a number written in a feminine flow.

"You get a girl's number, Dawson?" I joke, choosing to slide the napkin out of the way instead of trashing it.

"Shit. Yeah." Cash reaches then stuffs the thin paper cloth into his front jeans pocket. "Got a date. To a wedding."

"To a *wedding*?" I laugh, typing in my information and sliding the credit card when prompted.

"Yep. It started out kinda like a joke, so maybe I won't go but... Got the girl's number. We'll see."

On the one hand, I think he's crazy for accepting a random date—never mind a date *to a wedding*—from some woman he helped while working tonight, but on the other...

I think of Sophia.

And if she were to text me back and say she'd love to hang out on Monday...

I'd probably jump for joy, not gonna lie.

The night is winding down, and while you can hear the partying happening out on the street, the majority of the people in O'Gallaghers now are our late night, closing-time regulars. As patrons leave, and staff does too, it begins to feel like any other Saturday night—just with a giant leprechaun on the wall, mooning the establishment.

When one a.m. rolls around and Cash clocks out, we're down to four patrons. Two are playing dice. One is on his phone. The other is throwing cash down on the pine and pushing away from his spot at the bar.

"Have a good night, Cory," I say, lifting my hand in his direction.

"Good night, Jake," he answers back. I gather his money and the empty glass.

Saint is in the back finishing up back-of-house cleaning and throwing the mop around the floor. The cooks are good about closing down the fryers and grills, but there are final dishes to run, floors to clean, and random stock to organize every night. As long as we remain calm out here—knock on wood—he can get the back in closing shape.

I clean the front as I'm able and with these three particular patrons, I have no doubt Saint and I will get out of here on time tonight. They'll all leave between one forty-five and two. We can lock up. Clean the tables and floors.

And be out by two-thirty.

For being the busiest night of the year, we're in good shape.

It's one-forty when one of the dice players announces he's ready to head home. "Let me get you closed out," I say, leaving my towel on the bar to turn toward the register. I find his digital tab and print it off. Typically he has us use the card we hold, but I ask all the same.

Permission granted, I swipe for payment and bring the card, two copies of the receipt, and a cheap BIC pen to him.

"You, too, Jim?" I ask, going back to pull the second man's tab.

"Sure, just ring it through. Give the tip bucket a twenty and we're good." He'll still sign the slip, but I get him fully squared away on the computer end.

When they're gone, I look over to the single patron who remains in the establishment. "You want one more before I start shutting things down, Greg?" With only one customer, there's no need for an official last call announcement.

Greg has to be in his late fifties, although I think he's retired so maybe he's older. I don't know much about him even though he comes in a few nights a week. He's not one to open up.

"Please. Then I'll get out of your hair and maybe you and Saint can get out of here on time," he chuckles, the sound rough.

"No need to rush. You've got time," I tell him, placing the ice-cold pint in front of him.

I'm wiping down liquor bottles and the shelves they're displayed on when I hear the swoosh as the main door opens from outside. My initial instinct is to look at the time. It's one-fifty-three. Legally, we cannot sell alcohol after two, so the person is cutting it close.

I'm exhausted and not in the mood to deal with a

belligerent patron, so I put up a quick prayer that it's an easy person. With a practiced grin on my face, I turn to greet the late newcomer.

My fake smile morphs into a real one at who I see.

Sophia glances at Greg quickly as she slides onto a barstool smack in the middle of the bar. "I thought I'd keep you company. Is that allowed?"

Schooling my expression to not be a total creeper who's excited she came back, I answer as calmly as I can, "Sure. Absolutely." Unlike earlier when her hair was down, now Sophia's light locks are piled on top of her head in a messy bun. Her face is free of makeup and she wears my sweatshirt from Thursday night.

She's fucking beautiful.

She looks like mine.

"You want something to drink? Can't sell alcohol after two." Out of habit, I place a cocktail napkin down in front of her.

"Just water is okay."

She sips on the offered ice water and within minutes, it's just her, me, and Saint. I lock the front door behind Greg as Saint comes to the front, propping open the swinging door for closing.

"You got floors out here, Jake? Oh. Hey. Um..."

As I start to put chairs on tables at the far end of the room, I make introductions. "Saint, this is my neighbor, Sophia. Sophia, Max St. James."

"You were manning the doors earlier when me and my friend came down," Sophia's voice carries. Wanting to get all the chairs up, I continue my task while keeping an eye on the two. Saint is still standing in the door frame, a slightly confused, comical look on his face as he looks at her.

"Yeah, yeah. I remember you." His look of confusion turns toward me now, brows in the air.

With my own eyes wide and brows up, I tip my head toward the back, hoping he gets the hint to leave.

Saint's face relaxes and he steps toward the register. "I'll get the register closed up and finish back-of-house inventory. Holler if you need anything."

Once again, it's just me and Sophia.

"How's that water?" I ask, putting up the last of the chairs.

"Refreshing," she answers, turning on the stool to face me. She places her hands between her knees, pressing them together. "Almost as good as Starbucks water."

"Don't tell me you're one of those people who say all water tastes different," I laugh.

"It does! Some are super chemical-y. Most definitely reverse osmosis. Some are thick."

"I've never had a thick glass of water."

"Not like, thick-thick. But just, they *taste* thick."

"That's..." I stop myself from saying it's weird, and instead, use the word, "different."

Instead of going on about the water, she turns again on the stool, her gaze following me as I walk to the backside of the bar. "You're sure it's okay that I'm here? I didn't know what closing entailed and thought I could return the favor. Walk you home, if you'd walked."

"And return my sweatshirt?" I tease.

She glances down and then back at me. "I was debating keeping it, to be honest."

"You could." It was in high school I learned when you give a girl your sweatshirt, the likelihood of getting it back was slim.

A guy only shares when he's okay if it doesn't ever return to his closet.

And knowing Sophia has something of mine...

Not a hardship.

When she doesn't respond, I continue with the small talk that doesn't feel awkward. "Did you walk back by yourself?" Just because the crowds have been busy and the streets are a party, doesn't mean it's any safer for someone to walk in the earliest hours of the morning.

"I carry Mace®," is her non-answer, as she moves to dig her keys out of the right pocket of my sweatshirt. She pulls out a fabric loop, shaking it gently. The keys and charms jangle, and a thick turquoise tube swings just below them. I know for a fact she didn't have that the other night. She may be using it as an excuse that she's safe to walk, but I know it's not an always-on-her-person kind of thing.

Meaning, if the event came where she'd need to use it, she may not remember she has it.

Or, worse, she goes for it and she *doesn't* have it.

The need to scold her for walking alone—even with the pepper spray—is strong.

I don't bother berating myself for feeling protective over this particular woman.

I wouldn't say I'm the guy who rescues damsels in distress. It's not that I'm attracted to women who appear weaker.

Quite the opposite.

Watching my younger sister go through what she did, and become the woman she is now? I know that women aren't the weaker sex. I've seen it with my own eyes.

Sophia doesn't strike me as weak.

Did she have a weak moment?

Sure. But we all have them.

And let's just put it out there—I was caught by her beauty well before I knew why she'd been down the other night.

"But to save you from the impending coronary attack I see happening behind your eyes," she waves two pointed fingers in my direction, as if circling what she sees, "Emina dropped me off."

A sudden calm washes over me at her words. "I thought she goes to bed early." I desperately want to just stand by the bar and talk to her but I also know the longer I stand around, the later Saint and I will get out.

If only out of respect for my closing partner, I know I have to keep working.

Usually when closing, I mop the floors before running the last of the glassware, but I switch it up tonight so I have an excuse to be near Sophia and continue our conversation.

"She does. But this was her idea."

"This?"

"Coming back tonight. Giving you company on your way home. Bringing back your sweatshirt."

Chuckling, I place glasses on the blue crate that will go in the glassware washer. After this load, I'll have to clean the machine too.

"Ah, you're the type to evade and avoid, aren't you?"

"When embarrassed? Abso-freaking-lutely."

Even though I like that she doesn't hold back, I scrunch my brows, glancing up at her while placing glasses on the crate. "What's to be embarrassed about?" At least she has a half-grin on her face.

"One," she puts her elbow on the bar and lifts a finger. "I'm not the girl who gets *that* wasted. I'm not a big drinker to begin with, and if I'm going to drink, I prefer to do it in my comfies while on my couch."

"Your comfies?" There's no stopping the tease.

Her half-smile fills and her eyes brighten. "Yes, my comfies. Pajamas. Sweats. The likes."

"I figured that's what they were. Just haven't heard them labeled that way."

"It's because they're comfortable. Comfy."

"Yeah, I got that," I chuckle. "Two?"

"I'm sorry?"

"You were counting the reasons why you're embarrassed. You gave me one, what's the second?" I bend to place the crate in the washer, then glance around the bar for any other random glasses. The only glass that remains is Sophia's but leaving one or two dishes in the industrial-sized sinks in the kitchen isn't a big deal.

"Oh, yes. Two." She holds up a second finger. "I... Never mind." She brings her hand back down to her lap.

Grinning, I lean into the bar, my hands backward as I gasp the edge. "No, tell me. What's two?"

She regards me for what feels like thirty long seconds before she shrugs and looks down. "If I recall correctly, I shared the reason why I was in the state I was in."

"Josh."

Her eyes snap to mine again and I shrug a shoulder, pushing away from the bar. "I have a decent memory." She used his name in a passing comment but it stuck out to me.

Again, I have to tamper down the protective urges that course through me.

"Listen, Soph," I say, double-checking the condiments and making sure everything has date stickers. "If anyone should be embarrassed, it's the asshole who cheated. Not you. That said, probably wasn't the smartest thing to go get wasted after finding out but I'm glad someone was there for you."

"You."

"Your roommate, too," I try brushing off. "But...anyone here would have done the same."

"Walked me home?"

"Or gotten you into an Uber."

"I don't like—"

"Riding with strangers." I wink at her. "You said."

"I left nothing to the imagination, did I?"

"Oh. Definitely plenty left to the imagination," I answer, leaving her at the bar to grab the mop bucket from the kitchen.

My imagination has run rampant since leaving her in her bedroom on Thursday night. I don't make it a habit to walk patrons home.

Sophia is the first.

She may very well be the last.

I don't know what prompted me to do it but making sure she got home safely was important to me that night.

Then carrying her through her townhome to her bedroom...

I can still feel her in my arms.

More than all of that combined though, is the memory of her nightstand. When looking for a piece of paper to write on, I tried there first.

Sure, I found a small notebook and a pen, which I used.

But I'd also found a silicone, magenta, dick-shaped vibrator.

So yeah. My imagination has been in overdrive where Sophia's concerned.

I've imagined that fake dick between her legs.

Or better, *me* between her thighs while teasing her with the vibrations.

My thoughts surrounding Sophia haven't all been of a sexual nature though.

I'd been positive that the next time I'd see her—if ever—would be at the complex. I'd contemplated spending time at each of the three pools, wasting minutes in the mail room, and even taking Boo on extra long walks, all in hopes to get a glimpse of her again.

To get a chance to speak to her once more.

She's beautiful, sure, but while I don't understand why she effects me the way she does, I *know* I'd get along with her well. She'd been reserved in comparison to her friends when I first met her.

More open, a touch sad, when I met her the second time that same night.

Completely open and unabashed when I walked her home.

The multiple sides to Sophia I saw on Thursday alone, paired with the knowledge that some asshole cheated on her, had me imagining what I'd do to keep a woman like her.

And then she walked into O'Gallaghers today.

My mind completely on the woman at the bar, I don't notice when Saint steps out of the office.

"She came back."

I turn off the hoses that are in the yellow mop bucket, filling it with fresh cleaning water.

"She did," I state the obvious, pulling the bucket on wheels out of the water dump station.

"You like her."

"Don't know her." I grab the mop from where it's placed in a clip and drop it into the bucket.

"You lie so fucking bad," Saint chuckles but thankfully, he doesn't continue to push that particular angle. "I'm almost done back here. You getting work done or do we need to switch?"

I know he's just being an ass, so I give him my middle finger. "I just need to do the floors and then I'm done up front. We'll get out on time."

He taps the door jam with both open hands—*bah-dah-boom*—and turns back into the office, and I roll the mop bucket to the front of house. Sophia's attention is focused on the one television that is still on but at this hour, all that's playing are infomercials.

"Have they convinced you you need one yet?" I ask, rolling the bucket past her and toward the middle of the room.

"Doesn't everyone need a puppy pad for the bed?"

I glance at the screen and see a man holding a large towel-like piece of fabric in front of him. In large yellow letters, the screen declares it "absorbs liquid without ruining your mattress."

"That's not for puppies, Sophia," I chuckle, squeezing the excess water from the mop head before walking toward the dart boards.

"I'm aware."

I have a feeling she's blushing, so I check over my shoulder.

Even from across the room, I can see the pink in her cheeks.

"Yeah, so, anyway," Sophia says with a short cough. "Am I walking you home tonight?"

"Would you get in my truck if I told you I drove?"

"I would."

"Ah, so we're not strangers anymore?" I grin, moving the mop back and forth over the floor.

"You're a step up from a stranger."

"Only one step?" I rinse the mop and dip it in the water again, cleaning the next section of the floor.

"Eh. Maybe two."

I could get used to this banter with her.

"I walked today. Thought it would be safer with all the Irish ale and green beer flowing freely through the streets."

Sophia's laugh is light. "Funny. Emina and I had the exact opposite thought. We drove this afternoon and then again tonight because we thought there'd be more assholes on the road, and no one wants to be the victim of a car driving on the sidewalk."

"Well then, it's a good thing you thought to walk me home. Keep me safe," I joke and thankfully, she laughs again.

Yeah.

I could get used to this.

EIGHT

"HERE." Jake stands beside me and offers his hand.

I take it, grinning at the absurdity. "I can walk on a wet floor just fine, Jake." Absently, I reach for my water glass.

"Better safe than sorry."

"You just wanted to hold my hand." I'm not sure what's come over me. This flirty side isn't one I relate to.

But he makes it so dang easy.

I expect him to make a joke right back, but he doesn't. Instead, he squeezes my hand. "Is that okay?"

My body warms when he doesn't deny it. "It is," I confess, allowing him to walk me through the doorway leading to the kitchen.

"I just need to mop behind the bar. It'll just be a minute." Jake releases my hand and points somewhere behind me. "There's a stool there if you want to sit. Or I can get Saint to bring a chair out from the office."

"I'm fine. Can I put this somewhere?" I hold up the near-empty water glass.

"The sinks are right over there. The left is for things that need to be washed."

"Would you like me to wash it? I can."

Jake shakes his head, an amused, half grin under the day-old scruff lining his jaw and chin. Gosh, I really like his grin.

He gets deep lines beside the upturned cheek that nearly reach the long lines that appear by his eyes.

Even with a partial smile, he smiles with his entire face.

"Just put it in the sink. It's fine."

Trusting him, and realizing there are far more tubes and things going into the sink then I'd be able to figure out on my own, I place the glass in the deep tub and move to stand in the middle of the small alley-like way. Arms crossed, I look around.

Upon closer inspection, I see the sink is actually a trio of them, with signs saying which of the three serves which purpose in the rinse-clean-rinse process. Directly opposite is a space for food prep and cooking. Everything appears to be wiped down and cleaned, ready for tomorrow.

There's a large metal door that I'm guessing is the fridge or freezer, but when I notice there's only one door, I assume it must be both somehow.

On the walls are large laminated posters, all with different purposes.

One is about kitchen safety. Another has O.S.H.A. in large block letters and fine print underneath.

A smaller sign has a diagram of the tables and bar, with a dry-erase marker hanging on a shoestring from a push pin. I imagine that's what tells each person which section of the room they're in charge of when serving.

Finding things to read on the walls, I can hear Saint. I'm guessing he's in the office which must be around the corner. There's music playing lightly but it's the only obvious sound in the establishment.

Then it's the sound of the mop bucket rolling that has me looking toward Jake re-entering the back. He grins at me as he pushes the bucket and mop and I step out of the way.

"Still doing okay?"

"I am." The thought that I may have overstepped by appearing right before closing hits but Jake isn't making me feel unwanted in the slightest. Not that I'll be making a habit of coming at close.

I don't think, anyhow.

I watch as he dumps the mop water into what looks like a base of a shower stall, then rinses out the bucket before placing it upside down, wheels up, in the area. He pushes the mop handle into a grip while looking somewhere I can't see. I'm guessing the office.

"Front's done. Anything else back here need to be done?"

"Nope," Saint's voice answers, and the music he was playing stops. "Actually, I didn't grab the tip glass. Want to drop those in the safe, and label them for the last two hours? I'll be finished in thirty seconds."

Once again, I take a step out of the way when Jake comes near. He surprises me by holding out his hand in a familiar gesture, brushing my hip as he moves past. Instead of coming back right away, he pulls open a drawer under the register, producing a clear poly bag along with a Sharpie marker. I watch as he reaches into the large, handled beer glass they use for tips, removing dollar bills and organizing them.

"You're pretty awake for this hour," he mentions, his eyes remaining on task. "What do you do for work?"

"I don't work third shift, if that's what you're wondering. I took a nap before coming back."

Jake chuckles and looks at me this time.

Shrugging, I add, "I'm not much of a night person."

"Not a night person. Not a drinker. But here you are. Past closing time at a pub."

"I think we covered the reason for that." Afraid he'll somehow turn the subject, I answer his original question. "I do video editing for social media influencers and families who do video blogging."

"Like for YouTube?"

"And TikTok, Instagram... Facebook."

He dumps what remains in the glass—coins—in the clear envelope. "That sounds interesting."

"It's fun. Pays the bills." I've never been insecure about my chosen career but I suddenly worry it's not a good enough job.

I mean, I get paid well.

Both of my family content creators pay my standard $50-an-hour rate, with additional pay when I break down a twenty-minute video into two or three shorts for YouTube, or pieces that can be published on TikTok or Instagram and Facebook.

I'm usually given an entire day's worth of content to go through and edit, sometimes as many as fourteen hours of footage to trim down into a more digestible, twenty-minute piece.

There's an art to editing content, too. You can't just give little pieces of a day and push it together, calling it a video.

You have to tell a story.

There has to be something in the family's day that will keep a viewer watching until the end.

Thankfully, neither family has chosen an immediate turnaround, where they film one day and post the next. Most families who release videos on that tight of a schedule do their own editing, for the sake of time.

One of my families works on a three-day schedule—I'll get Monday's content late Monday night, edit it on Tuesday with wiggle room into Wednesday, for them to post on Thursday. That family also only posts three times a week, on Tuesday, Thursday, and Saturday.

And because their vlog-life is essentially timeless, if the family isn't doing anything on Monday but had a fun-filled weekend, my Monday content will be of the previous weekend.

My other family is a full week ahead in their content schedule, but they post daily, Monday through Saturday. Monday's footage will be posted the following Monday.

My busiest days are the ones where I have both families to edit, but because they've been posting on the same sched-ules for the entire two years I've worked with them, I have my process down pat.

It also helps that they're both really good about telling me if there's a specific event they want highlighted in their video, which gives me a game plan before I open the files.

"Any divas?" Jake teases, ripping off the piece of paper that kept the bag from sealing on itself.

"No. I have great clients."

This time when Jake walks toward me, he reaches for a panel and the lights in the pub dim, leaving the front of O'Gallaghers blanketed in black. Even the neon signs in the window go dark.

"We'll leave out the back door," he explains. "You can follow me. Just need to drop this in the safe."

Walking behind him, I take in more of the kitchen that I wasn't able to see from my stance before. Around the corner is where the office is, and there's another open area where metal shelves hold paper goods and shelf-stable cans.

When he steps into the office, I stay just outside the doorway.

"Finished," he announces, walking to an under-desk safe beside Saint. Jake opens a drawer in the top, places the clear envelope inside, then pushes the drawer closed, open, then closed again. In between the heavy sounds of the drawer slamming in and out, I hear the coins in the envelope hit the bottom of the safe.

Saint finger-pecks into the laptop keyboard before closing the screen. "We're good here too. I'll go set the alarm."

Jake and I move to one of the two doors in the back as Saint jogs to the front, then back toward us again. "Set."

It's only then that Jake opens the back door, holding it for both me and Saint, who hits another set of lights, dousing the back-of-house in near darkness—all but for the soft glow of a single light in the middle of the room. Once everyone's out, Saint locks the door with a key on what I'd guess is his regular keychain.

Just outside the door we exited, is another door to the pub's right, hardly a foot between the two. "Does that door go with the second door inside?" I ask, curious.

"There's an apartment upstairs. Usually Rory and Emily use it when they're in town," Saint explains.

"Ah."

"When do you work next?" Saint asks Jake as we all step away from the building.

"Tuesday. You?"

"Tonight," he groans, sending his keys on a full rotation around his finger, catching them against his palm. "Off Monday and Tuesday. Wednesday?"

"Yep. I'll be here."

My eyes dart between the two men as they discuss their schedule in short hand.

"Cool. See you then." The other man holds his hand up in a wave. "It was nice to officially meet you, Sophia."

"You too, Saint," I reply before stuffing my hands in the pockets of Jake's sweatshirt. Taking my cues from the one I came to see, I wait until he takes a step toward the front of the building and begin walking beside him.

Suddenly, I'm unsure how to proceed so I go with trusty ol' small talk. "How long have you worked at O'Gallaghers?"

"Just about a year." As we head west, there's an oncoming group traveling our way, talking and laughing, paying little attention to what's going on around them. Jake smoothly pulls me behind him, holding onto my hand, as we pass the crew, forcing them closer to the road while we practically hug the buildings. Some shoulders are bumped but once we've made it by, Jake resumes walking beside me, keeping me on the inside and dropping my hand. "I moved into the townhomes after college and was looking for work. Heard good things about the O'Gallagher siblings and how they run their business."

I guess I wasn't prepared to hear he'd gone to college. "What did you go to school for?"

"English major. I have a degree that I don't know what to do with." His chuckle is bordering on self-deprecating.

"Tell me about it," I grin. "I went to school for business

and learned quickly I have zero business—no pun intended—manning a business."

"But you're basically running a business now though, right?"

"Well, sure, but it's different."

"Is it, though? You're the one making all the decisions. If you need work, you're the one making those connections. You make financial decisions."

I shrug a shoulder. "I guess it was always drilled in my head that my degree should be used in some big Fortune 500 company, and not some little LLC that I run."

"By who, your parents?" He sounds offended on my behalf.

"A little." I hold up a hand, "But they're great parents. They were originally worried my choice of work was going to put me in severe debt. They're a different generation. All of this internet work is foreign to them."

"I guess."

Curious about this particular topic, I ask, "Are your parents upset that you have a degree you don't use?"

"Nah. They're just happy I graduated," Jake laughs. "My sisters were always the overachievers and I barely scraped by with Cs."

"Tell me about your family?"

"Well, I have my parents. Dad was a mechanic when we were growing up. My mom was a homemaker, and when all of us kids were in school full-time, she started to do odd jobs at the schools. I have two younger sisters. Chandler is twenty-two and Hollis is twenty."

"They certainly got the cool names," I joke good-heartedly.

"What, you don't like Jake?" he jokes right back.

"No! No, I don't mean it like that." My smile is wide as

I glance at him. "It's a good name. You're definitely a Jake. But yours is so…"

"Normal?"

"Yeah."

"To be fair, my name is legally Jacobi."

"Ahh. So you have a fun name too, after all."

"I do, I do." We're nearing the bridge, and I'm not surprised when he teases, "You going to make it over okay tonight?"

"Ha, ha." I do, however, take my hands out of the sweatshirt pockets. "Emina and I have talked about how dangerous this bridge can be if you're intoxicated."

"Considering you beefed it the other night, yeah, I'd say so." We're both quiet as we walk over the foot bridge, the sound of our feet on the engineered planks reverberating against the water underneath. It's only after we're off the bridge that our conversation picks up again. "Do you have siblings?"

Shaking my head, I put my hands back in the pockets. "Nope. Only child. Although Emina's like a sister to me. She's been my person since college."

"So you two are close?"

"Very. Are you close to your family? Your sisters?"

"We are, except for physical distance. My family's in Montana."

"Did school bring you to California, then?"

"It did. I like the weather. Haven't felt like taking back true winters yet," he chuckles. "So much snow."

I can't help but mirror his laugh. "I grew up here. Well, not here, here, but in Temecula. It's about an hour and a half north. Ish."

"I've heard of the city but have never been."

"They have some neat wineries and resorts," I offer. I'm

not the best person when it comes to hyping up her hometown.

"That you've never been to?"

When I look over at him, I see the smirk on his face.

"Just because I'm not a big drinker doesn't mean I *never* drink," I say around my own smirk. "I like a nice red wine, thank you very much."

"We don't sell a lot, but we have been known to have wine on the premises."

"I'll keep that in mind."

I swear, our stride slows the closer we get to the townhome apartment complex. We talk about everything and nothing. It's an easy conversation that has me feeling lighter than I've felt in a long time.

"You said you're in the first phase?" I ask when Jake holds open the gate door for me. He follows behind, making sure it closes securely behind us. The sound of the door's automatic lock sounds before he answers.

"I am. Building three."

I look up at the giant placard at the top center of the nearest building. It's number two.

"I suppose I should get this back to you, then." I reach for the pull, intending to unzip the warm cotton that surrounds me.

"I'll walk you back to your place."

"No, it's okay...really." Reluctantly, I begin to unzip.

Jake steps to stand in front of me, putting his hand on top of mine, halting the downward motion. "Let me walk you home, Soph. Please."

The way he stands so near...

His hand on top of mine...

Those amber brown eyes locked with mine...

And when he tugs the zipper back up...

My heart starts beating to a faster cadence and I swallow hard to try and calm my sudden nerves.

Needing to find solid ground, I attempt to tease but even to my ears, it falls flat. "I thought I was walking *you* home tonight."

His knuckles trail down my stomach ever so lightly, as he slowly drops his hand to grasp mine. "Let me walk you home."

"Okay."

His hand completely engulfing mine has me thinking dirty thoughts. His fingers are thick as the weave around my own. I wonder what they'd feel like against more the more sensiti—

Sophia!

Clearing my throat, I glance over at him swiftly but he's looking ahead as we stroll through the complex.

"You have off tomorrow? Or, well, today, I guess? What do you usually do on your days off? I'm sure you sleep until noon."

"I can't sleep in," he chuckles. "It's practically impossible. My internal clock will always wake me up at six."

"Oh, that's super early. Especially after working so late."

"Drove my mom crazy growing up."

"I am definitely a sleeper-inner. My mom hated it," I laugh. "I'd have a lacrosse tourney that kept me out until midnight on a Friday, and I'd try sleeping until mid-afternoon on Saturday. She'd be knocking on the door, *C'mon, Soph, we've got errands to run!*"

He chuckles at my story. "I take it she didn't sleep in?"

"Nope. Said you lost too much of the productive day by sleeping during morning hours. I mean... I get it. The world works on a nine-to-five schedule. But... I love my bed."

I'm going to blame the hour for the way my mind once again goes dirty, now thinking about Jake in my bed.

I don't know what it is about this man that has me feeling so...

Free.

Even when I rushed into things with Josh, being with him didn't feel like *this*.

Like my soul recognizes his.

Which is ridiculous. I just met the man.

He was kind and walked me home one night.

...And then I gave in to the girly desire to put myself in his space and return the favor.

Maybe he's just being kind.

But "kind" guys don't hold your hand.

They don't put you in your bed, and leave you there with a note, locking up the house behind them.

Kind guys put you in a rideshare and wish you well.

"You have videos to edit today?" Jake interrupts my thoughts.

"I do. It usually takes me a couple of hours."

"Depending on when you finish, maybe you, Emina, Ben, and me could hang out at one of the pools."

"That could be fun. Only one is heated though, right? The one by the leasing office? I'm not about that cold water life."

"I think so." I can hear the smile in his tone.

"I'll bring it up to Em. See what she says. But I'm open to it, for sure."

"Great."

"Just...not at seven in the morning. Maybe around noon or something."

Laughing, Jake nods. "That works. But don't let me

disturb your work. Text me when you wake up and have an idea of time."

"Sounds like a plan."

We're standing outside my gate now, and as much as I don't want to say goodbye yet, I can't stifle the yawn that breaks through. "Gosh, I'm sorry," I say, holding my hand in front of my mouth.

"Guess that nap was only a little helpful," Jake jokes, and I nod, lowering my hand to my side once again.

"I don't know how you do it. Work this late."

"You get used to it."

Before I can bring my hands back to the zipper, Jake stops me yet again. "Keep it."

"Jake..."

"Give me a reason to see you again."

"I'll see you this afternoon."

"A reason to see you after today."

I attempt to stare him down, but then I'm yawning again and he laughs at me.

Not the picture of intimidating, I guess.

"Keep the hoodie." He reaches around my body to lift the metal that keeps my gate closed, before pushing it open behind me. "Good night, Soph."

I take a step back into the confines of my unit's so-called yard.

"Good night, Jake."

"Thank you for walking me home."

There's amusement in his tone, so I answer it with my own. "Glad to return the favor."

He starts closing the gate between us—and I'm not sure what comes over me. I slap a hand out to stop the progress. In an awkward move, I take a step toward him, go up on tip toes, and press my lips to his.

I don't give it time to become something other than a light kiss.

Except Jake has different ideas.

Before I can fully pull away, he wraps a hand around the back of my neck, dragging me into a deeper kiss. The hand not on my neck is now on the small of my back, pressing, pressing, pressing, until I step as close to him as I possibly can.

My hands are on his body, one on his chest and the other on his side. Curling my fingers, I have fistfuls of shirt.

He tastes faintly of mint and cola, and with the way his mouth commands mine, all other thoughts cease.

His thumb gently sweeps up and down along the side of my neck. When I mew against his mouth, his lips curl and he pulls away. He adjusts his hand so his thumb can brush against my lower lip. I watch as his eyes track the movement before lifting to meet mine.

"Good night, Soph," he murmurs. He releases his hold of me at the same time he presses another small kiss to my forehead, and takes a step back.

I'm stuck in place.

With a dark chuckle, Jake nods up toward my door. "Go inside before I ask to take that further."

"I... you..."

"I'll see you this afternoon."

I swallow before licking my lips. I can still taste him. "Okay. I'll... I'll see you later."

It takes everything in me to turn and step toward my front door, pushing the buttons to unlock it. I look over my shoulder to see him standing by the gate, although it's closed between us now.

"Good night, Jake."

"Good night, Soph." But before the front door can click shut, he calls out again. "Hey, Sophia?"

I lean against the open door. "Yeah?"

"Don't bring that hoodie with you later."

I have a flirty response on the tip of my tongue but it wars with confusion and lust. Instead, I just nod. "Okay. I won't."

NINE

I TELL Ben the plans I made for us when we're getting in a morning workout at the complex's gym.

"The roommate is the one with the super curly hair, right?" Ben asks, re-racking his weights.

"Yeah. Emina." I grab my keys from the cube-storage system that is used a personal storage. "I figured we'd grill and shit. I'm going to head to the grocery store, grab some things. You want anything specific?"

He shakes his head, picking up the bottled water he brought and taking a swig. "Nah. Whatever you pick up is good."

Two hours later, it's only ten and I'm itching to hear from Sophia. I'm sure she's sleeping.

Or working.

But I'm antsy to see her again.

She'd surprised me last night by initiating our kiss. I probably should have let her have her little kiss and been happy with it. I should have stopped myself from giving in to the urge to claim her mouth with mine.

Except I did take the kiss further—and I haven't been able to think of anything else since.

The way her body felt under my hands...

The way her tongue slipped and swirled against mine...

The way her small moan sent a thrill through my entire body, sending my dick into high alert...

I replayed that sound as I fisted myself in bed, imagining her bare body on top of me, riding my cock until we both lost ourselves in oblivion.

I have to keep reminding myself she's coming out of another relationship. I don't know enough about it—whether it had been a short one or one that lasted years—but the last person I want to be is her rebound.

Rebounds never last.

It's that age-old adage: *the best way to get over someone is to get under someone else.*

That said... I'm not going to let that stop me from getting to know her a little better.

I'm lounging on the couch with one of Ben's strays, Mike, when there's a ruckus coming from the kitchen. It sounds like Boo is getting into something she shouldn't be.

After depositing the large gray cat onto the couch—he gives a dissatisfied meow—I check out what my dog is up to.

"What are you doing, Boo?" I ask, stepping around the peninsula counter. She looks up from where she had her head nosing through a plastic bag from the grocery store.

Her ears aren't cropped but one stands up more often than not, as it is now.

With one ear up and the other folded back, and those big blue puppy dog eyes she's mastered, I can almost hear her telling me she's doing nothing. Absolutely nothing.

"There's nothing in there for you, girlfriend."

She wags her butt—because it's not enough to just move her tail—and plops to sit, offering me a paw as I step closer.

Grinning, I give her paw a shake before patting her head. "Let me find you a cookie."

The moment I open the cupboard door that houses all the treats for the four-legged creatures, it's not just Boo in the kitchen.

We're joined by Sully and Mike, as well as two kittens Ben hasn't named yet. For now, they're Thing One and Thing Two.

It's a freaking zoo in here.

After giving Boo a dog biscuit, I lay out a few treats for Mike and the Things, before scooping up Sully.

Sully is fat, fluffy, and white.

He's also blind.

While he's not the first cat Ben rescued from the stray life—those two are now living with Shayne—Sully *is* the first one that Ben decided to keep. Since then, the cats just keep appearing. He'll be finding homes for the Things, but the Monsters, Inc. Crew is here to stay.

Putting Sully on top of his cat tree, I place five treats in front of him. "There you go, man. But hurry up. The Things won't be occupied for long."

From the couch, my phone rings in a generic tone. After scratching the cat's head one last time, I head to pick it up. I'm not fancy and don't differentiate my ringer for phone calls or incoming text messages.

It's always a surprise, I say.

This time, it's a text message.

SOPHIA:

Good morning. Do you still want to meet up today?

ME:

Absolutely. I have things for the grill.

SOPHIA:

Okay. Em has a meeting at 4 so I think noon would work best for us. Is that okay for you guys?

ME:

We're ready when you are.

We confirm which pool we're meeting at—the heated one in the front of the complex—and at what time—noon.

Looking at the clock, I figure I'll head down to the pool by quarter to noon to claim a grill but I have a little more than an hour to waste.

Something tells me it's going to be the longest hour in history.

I FEEL good about this girl.

Two hours at the pool came and went. The four of us ate burgers and hung out, spending some time in the hot tub too, although when Ben brought up playing a game of chicken in the water, Emina quickly shut it down because of her upcoming meeting.

Ben walked Emina to the girls' place and Sophia stayed behind with me to clean the remnants of our fun afternoon.

"Did you get work done earlier?" I ask, throwing away

the last of our garbage as Sophia places condiments in the cooler I rolled down.

"I did." She shuts the lid and does another look around. "I have probably an hour or so left to do with one family but I don't have to turn their edited piece over until tomorrow at noon. I have some time still."

"You maybe want to hang out some more? Maybe find a movie or something on TV?" I couldn't tell you the last time I went about asking a girl out in what my parents would call a normal way.

These days, it's all apps and swiping left or right.

Grabbing drinks and taking a rideshare to someone's house for a few hours of added fun.

I swear, the last time I asked a girl out the "old-fashioned way" was probably in high school.

Sophia reaches for the crocheted coverup she had on when the girls got here and slips it over her head, the cream-colored knitted sheath not doing much to hide the black one-piece suit she wears.

"Sure. With Emina heading out for a meeting, maybe my place? That way we don't bother Ben?"

"He wouldn't care but yeah, that's fine. We can run this stuff back to my place, I'll change, and then we can head over to yours."

On our trek from mine and Ben's apartment to the girls' apartment, we pass Ben going in the opposite direction. He promises to walk Boo and after we've continued on our way, Sophia asks who Boo is.

"My dog. She's a white bully mix." When we'd stopped at my place, Sophia opted to wait for me outside, even when I told her she could come in. It was probably for the best though. Boo'd been excited to see me.

If she'd had the chance to meet a new friend, too, we wouldn't have made it out of the house.

And as much as I love Boo and the Crew, I'm looking forward to a couple hours of just me and Soph.

"I love dogs. We always had big dogs growing up, Danes...Dobies... but I just haven't felt settled enough to take on that responsibility."

"Well, if you ever want to get dog cuddles in, Boo's your gal. We also currently have four cats and they're all about that snuggle life."

Sophia stops dead in her tracks. "*Four* cats?"

Chuckling, I nod, taking her hand and pulling her along. "Ben rescues them. At first, it was funny. These random strays would gravitate toward him. Now it's pretty neat. He's kept two as his own, Mike and Sully. Then he's got two kittens that will get homes soon."

"Mike, Sully, and Boo?" Sophia's smile is wide.

"Yep. Mike, Sully, and Boo."

"For two grown men, I would have never pegged the two of you to have pets named after an animated movie."

"The kittens are Thing One and Thing Two," I add with a shrug. "Ben's mom is an elementary school teacher." I hope that makes sense to her because it makes sense to me.

"That's just the cutest thing I've ever heard, no lie. Never would have guessed it..."

At her townhome, we both remove our shoes at the door and head further in.

"Em? You still here?" Sophia calls out.

I look around their place, getting a better look now that it's daylight and not the middle of the night.

The bedroom door on this level is closed, but it's quickly pulled open. "Yeah. I'm heading out in a moment. Oh. Hey, Jake."

I nod and wave once.

"We're just going to hang out for a bit. I'm heading up to change and didn't want him to startle you if you were getting ready in your room. Jake, make yourself at home," Sophia turns toward me. "There's water and maybe a couple of sodas in the fridge. I'll be back down in a minute."

As Sophia runs up the stairs, Emina gives me a small, maybe awkward, smile before heading back into her room, leaving me in the middle of the open room by myself.

Unlike mine and Ben's bare walls, they have large canvas prints on theirs. They all look like they're in the same painting series, with rich blues, black, and gold speckling throughout. There's a vase of fresh flowers in the kitchen—some sort of colorful mix.

Momentarily, I wonder if the asshole ex sent them to Sophia but I quickly push the thought aside.

I'm almost certain Sophia isn't the type to entertain a cheater crawling back. Nor do I think she's the type to see two men at once.

In the living room portion of their apartment, they have an oversized, overstuffed, deep-seated couch.

It looks like one of those couches that engulfs you when you sit down.

Figuring this is where we're going to be hanging out, I give it a try.

And I nearly freaking moan at the comfort that surrounds me.

Thank God I stop myself, though, because Emina comes out of her room just about the same time the sound almost came out of my mouth.

Once again, she gives me that small, almost awkward, smile before grabbing her keys from the kitchen counter.

"I'm leaving, Soph!" she yells out before looking at me and saying, in a far normal decibel, "Bye, Jake."

I tell her bye back but as she's nearing the front door, I hear her say something not in English.

Russian, maybe?

One of those Slavic languages.

Part of me wants to ask what she said, but the other part is more interested in the sound of feet overhead as Sophia leaves her room and comes down the stairs.

"Bye, Em!" Sophia calls out just as the door opens and shuts.

"Your couch is really nice," I say when Sophia emerges from the stairs. Like me, she changed into more comfortable clothes.

But where I'm clothed in sweatpants and a tee shirt, she has on a long-sleeved shirt and short, cotton shorts.

Short shorts that show off her thick thighs and strong calves.

The legs of the shorts are big enough that I could easily slip my hands up and cup her ass.

Heaven help me.

I count to ninety-nine by threes to get my mind off how attractive I find this woman.

"Isn't it?" She grins at me and walks to the television console, coming back with a remote. She sits smack in the middle, bringing her legs up to sit cross-legged on the couch.

The couch is so deep, it may as well be called an extra-long, L-shaped twin-sized bed.

"It was my splurge purchase. We had an IKEA couch but I wanted a big girl couch, so I made it happen. You have any ideas on what to watch?"

We end up scrolling through all of her streaming services before settling on the new Knives Out movie.

"I'm warning you now," Sophia says, tossing the remote to the side of the couch I'm not sitting on. "I'm the type who watches whodunnits and mysteries and am vocal about trying to figure it out. I'm sorry in advance."

Anyone else, it's an annoying quality but sitting next to Sophia and watching her excitement as things unfold, I find it an endearing quirk.

Unfortunately, we're halfway through the movie when it buffers, then goes to the TV's equivalent of the Blue Screen of Death.

"No! This freaking TV..." Sophia leans over to grab the remote, presses a few buttons, and resets the television. After a minute, the TV restarts and she pulls up the movie again.

We're able to watch another twenty minutes before the TV freezes and needs to be restarted again.

"That freaking blows," Sophia mumbles.

"Does that always happen?"

She nods. "Has for the last few months. It's the TV we had in college and unfortunately, it just can't keep up with the times. Sometimes, it doesn't recognize it's connected to the internet."

"Splurge on a couch but not a television?" I joke.

"Neither of us watches a lot but we both enjoy lounging on the couch." She's not defensive in the slightest, which I appreciate.

Some females don't always catch teasing, but Sophia's been on the same wavelength as me every time I've thrown in a joke.

"Well, I guess I can go—"

"No! We have to finish the movie. Don't you want to know what happens? We'll pull it up on my laptop. C'mon.

I can't say my bed's as comfortable as the couch but we only have like...twenty minutes left."

I follow her upstairs to her room. Her bed is made and has a thousand—okay, only seven—pillows at the top, with a decorative throw over the lower corner. A vision of my bed comes to mind.

Pretty sure I haven't made it since I moved out of my parents' home.

The flat sheet may even be bunched at the foot.

The girls' entire apartment is in immaculate condition. Not a thing out of place.

Ben and I aren't slobs by any means, but there are more things out of place than in.

"Here." Sophia crawls up on her bed and sits back against her pillows before patting the open space beside her. "Pop a squat."

Doing as she requests, I sit beside her, letting my back sink into the pillows until I'm in an upright reclined position. "Do you sleep with all these pillows?"

She shakes her head as she pulls her laptop from the nightstand, setting it up on her lap. "No. Usually only one."

"Why do girls like so many pillows?" I tease, my eyes glancing around her bedroom, but avoiding the nightstand to my immediate right.

That's where her vibrator was the other night.

And fuck.

Just like that, I'm back to thinking about getting Sophia naked and exploring her body. The one-piece she wore to the pool did little to keep my mind off her silhouette, and now, in her bed... In the private confines of her room, where there's no question she pleases herself, there's no stopping the blood from traveling south, the telltale sign of my dick thickening evident.

Shit, I hope she doesn't look over.

Attempting to pull off the "getting comfortable" look, I bend my right knee and take one of the smaller, decorative pillows from behind me, putting it in my lap.

I'm fucking twenty-four years old.

I should be able to control myself a little better.

"All right. Here we go. Thank goodness the app saves where you were," Sophia mumbles, completely oblivious to my current state of peril.

We watch the last of the movie, but I'm paying little attention to it.

I can smell Sophia.

I can smell the spicy mint in her hair as she sits next to me, as well as on the pillows behind me. Anytime I shift my shoulders, the scent intensifies.

I can smell the sweet smell of her lotion as her shoulder presses to mine.

I've been in a state of half-arousal for nearly fifteen minutes and know it wouldn't take much for me to go full-staff.

Sweatpants were not the right call.

Comfortable or not.

"Gosh, that was fun," Sophia announces as the end credits roll. "And funny too."

Clearing my throat, I nod. "It was. Daniel Craig rarely disappoints."

"I'm not really a James Bond fan but I love a lot of his other work."

"So movie trivia nights, you wouldn't be helpful with 007 references. Got it."

"There's movie trivia night? Where? O'Gallaghers?"

Chuckling, I nod. "First Tuesday of the month."

"Are you allowed to play along, or do you usually work during?"

"Do you like trivia?"

"I do! I'm not great at it, but I like it," she says honestly, laughing, as she closes the laptop.

"I usually work those nights, but if you ever want to play, I could probably get someone to do a shift switch."

"Or I could just keep you company and listen in?" I hear the question in her statement, as she turns to replace the laptop on her nightstand.

As her hip lifts, the pillows behind her shift, and a flash of magenta catches my eye.

Her vibrator.

It's not in the drawer.

Which means it's probably been used recently.

Her legs splayed, that magenta dick head vibrating against her slick folds, making her wetter, wetter, wetter, until her body quakes against the mattress.

Fuck.

"I'd like—" I clear my throat against the sudden increase of arousal, "I'd like that. You keeping me company."

When she sits straight again, instead of leaning into the pillows, she turns to face me. Once again, her legs are criss-crossed in front of her and I have to fight the urge to look to her center. Do those wide short legs offer a peek of what's hidden beneath? Is she wearing underwear, or is she bare under the material?

I manage to keep my eyes on hers and notice as hers narrow slightly while she thinks.

"Thinking pretty hard, there."

Her hazel eyes dart away for a moment as she pinches her lips together, but then she's once again looking at me.

"I'm not the girl who hops around, man to man," she

explains. "I like to get to know a guy before I take it to the next step. I bent my rules with Josh and regretted it. Then, instead of being honest with me when I said I'd rather pump the brakes and slow down, he slept with my friends."

My cock deflates a little at the seriousness in her tone, but I'm still hard enough to keep the pillow firmly in my lap.

I adjust how I'm sitting though, fighting the need to grimace while remaining the picture of cool, calm, and collected.

"Soph—"

"...I also know, guys are different. Slow isn't the way most men operate. It's all, swipe left, swipe right, drinks, then fuck. But I'm just not built that way. I'm the girl who immediately wants long-term. I shouldn't admit that but... Might as well scare ya now so you can leave before things progress." The subdued nature of the comment borders between serious and a joke, but it also tells me she's ready to erect walls if needed.

"Sophia," I try again, reaching out to press my palm against her knee. When her shoulders slump from their tense, upward hold, I'm positive I have her attention. "It's not lip service when I tell you real men don't cheat. That's not me trying to get into your good graces and then your bed."

"You're in my bed." The fact she's teetering between serious and teasing is a good sign, I think.

I lift a brow and go with the racier term. "Between your legs," I spell out for her. "I'm more than happy taking things at your pace. Keeping each other company. Watching a movie now and then..." I think about her vibrator under her pillow, and as badly as I want to know if she thought of me while using it, I decide it's not a good time to bring it up.

"I'm not going anywhere, Soph. Take your time. You want to hang out just to hang out? I'm good for it. You want to keep me company at O'Gallaghers while I'm working? I'd be more than happy to see you there. You don't have to come when I close, though," I say with a chuckle. "That's late. I know it, you know it...there's no need for you to put yourself through the late hours and lack of sleep if you don't want to. You want to come to my place just for animal therapy? Ben and I have a zoo that would love your attention. Your pace. I'll be here." To make sure she understands, I add, "No plans on going anywhere else."

Her frown is back on her face, but it seems inquisitive this time. Her words surprise me—turns out, she's not oblivious, at all—but I'm starting to realize Sophia is the type of woman who will easily keep me on my toes.

"So even though you're hard," her eyes drop pointedly to my lap briefly, "you have no desire to take this further?"

I adjust the pillow but don't make a move to expose my tented sweats. "Desire? Yes. But I'm a grown man, Soph. Desire and acting on impulse are two different things."

"I was told I'm a tease." She holds eye contact while making the statement. I can see the statement bothers her.

She'd taken the words to heart.

With my hand still on her knee, a rub my thumb over the bare skin there in a comforting gesture. "I give as good as I get, Soph. You tease, I'm going to tease right back. I have no issue with it, just like I hope you wouldn't. But the moment you say stop, you say no... I will stop. Doesn't matter how hard it is...or I am," I wink at her to try and get her to smile, "I will stop. Okay?"

Her smile is slight but I can feel the relief coming off her. "Yes. Okay."

TEN

THIS GUY IS TOO good to be true.

When I brought him up to my room I wasn't thinking clearly.

I just wanted to watch the rest of the movie and didn't want to deal with unplugging my laptop, gathering the cord, bringing it downstairs, finding a nearby outlet, setting up the laptop again...

But the moment we were up here, it was *clear* how turned on Jake was.

I don't know what it was in my room that did it, but something made his sweatpants begin to tent and when he did the boy thing of putting a pillow on his lap, I knew.

I just knew.

And instantly got wet at the knowledge this man wants me.

The desire to put the movie aside and make out with

him—and get handsy—was strong but I cold-watered myself by remembering Josh.

The significant difference between my timeline with Josh and the one with Jake is I was tipsy the night Josh and I met. I may have swiped right and agreed to meeting when he messaged me back, but your girl needed to pregame to make sure she didn't make a fool of herself.

Yeah, yeah, I was drunk off my ass when things with Jake "started" but I first met him sober. The fact he knew who I was when Emina and I went back to O'Gallaghers...I was sober then.

In all honesty, all things considered, Josh probably had only been interested in a one-night stand, and sure, I'd been a willing participant, but I held on after. I asked him to do things. I invited him to get-togethers with the girls.

Because I'm not a one-night stand girl.

I need connection.

...Apparently, I force connection.

"You opposed to watching something else?" Jake cuts through my darkening thoughts. "Pop something up on your laptop over there, we can lay down... I'm a cuddler, and I think you could maybe use someone holding you. What do you say?"

"Well, that confirms it. You can't be real," I announce, the ease in which I can joke with him foreign. "You like to *cuddle*?" I work to hold back laughter.

"I do!" He doesn't look offended in the slightest. "And maybe I might need a nap, but I'm not ready to say goodbye yet. But if you'd rather I leave..." He makes a show of getting off the bed.

Yep, he's still hard, but not one hundred percent.

It's not easy to disguise any state of an erection behind

sweatpants, regardless of the color. Although gray does give you a nice outline when *not* hard.

"What do you want to watch?" I don't tend to fall asleep with new people around, but maybe I can get an hour or two of a funny sitcom in.

He stretches his legs out on the bed again. "Something mindless?"

"How about the show, Ghosts? It's silly and not something you have to pay close attention to. I have to catch up on this season."

"Sure. What's it about?"

I tell him about the premise—how a woman and her husband inherit a mansion, and after she hits her head, she can see and talk to the ghosts who inhabit the house, one of whom is an ancestor of hers. I also explain that it's the U.S. version and that I've caught some of the British episodes too. "British versions are usually far better, but I really like the U.S. one."

I start to bring the laptop to the bed but he waves me off. "Keep it there. Lay down with me?"

I didn't want to assume he was serious about laying down, but it looks like Jake speaks his mind. With the laptop on my nightstand, I angle it as Jake starts to remove pillows. I'm about to tell him he can just toss them anywhere when I realize he's dropping them—as neatly as one can—on the floor by his side.

I hit the space bar, the sitcom starting. After laying down, Jake pulls me to him, big spoon to my little spoon. My core pulses at the intimacy and I do my best to ignore it.

He has a hand on my stomach but keeps it over my shirt. Not sure what to do with my own hands, I end up putting one under my pillow and resting the other on top of his. Jake spreads his fingers until mine drop between his.

"TikTok would say you're a walking red flag," I quietly blurt out. I didn't mean to vocalize the words, but there you have 'em.

"Why? Because I want to hold you?"

"Because you're agreeable. This is like the honeymoon stage in dating. You're super nice and you listen, and you appear to care about my quirks—"

"Not wanting to have sex the moment you meet a person isn't a quirk, Soph," he answers softly, no heat in his words. "It's a respectable standard."

"I could get used to you being a nice guy," I say softly, risking a glance over my shoulder. He's staring at me, I realize when my eyes meet his. "Don't play with me."

He brushes a hair from my forehead before putting his arm back over my stomach, once again linking our fingers. "Wouldn't dream of it." His words sound sincere. I guess that's all I can ask.

I settle forward once again, adjusting my hand under my pillow...

And my fingers encounter silicone.

Hard.

Silicone.

The last few minutes flash before my eyes.

Earlier, all of my pillows were perpendicular to the bed.

Which means when Jake removed the pillows and put the remaining two down flat...

I swallow hard and try like hell to pay attention to the show playing, but I can't shut off my head.

Why, oh why, did I leave it there last night?

I always...

ALWAYS!

Clean up after playing. I wash my vibrator and put it back in its home in my nightstand.

Oh my God.

Not even Hetty and her Victorian-era snobbery banter with pant-less Trevor can pull me from the embarrassment flooding my body.

But apparently something the ghost says is funny because Jake silently chuckles behind me, the shaking of his chest a gentle vibration against my back.

It takes a little bit of time but I manage to calm enough where my heart isn't racing a million beats per second. Maybe he didn't see it. Maybe all the shuffling in the bed allowed it to remain hidden the whole time.

I could only be so lucky...

Eventually, Jake's soft snores catch my attention. He wasn't lying about needing a nap.

His arm is heavy over my side as he fully relaxes, the weight of which, paired with the soft brush of air coming from his parted lips, nearly lulls me to sleep, too.

I watch two episodes before succumbing to the need to close my eyes.

Falling asleep in his arms tells me everything I need to know about this man. In the short amount of time we've known each other, I trust him.

I miss an entire episode before I'm awoken by the short melodic title sequence between the cold open and first scene. With a sigh, I stretch my legs and arch my back slightly to not disturb Jake in case he's still sleeping.

Heck, asleep or awake, I'd rather not rub against him like a cat in heat.

Settling once more, I reach to hit a few buttons on my laptop, closing the streaming service and putting the device to sleep.

Before the screen blanks, I look at the time in small numbers. It's quarter to six. We'll have about another hour of sunlight before it gets dark, and I have some work to do yet. The moment the sun goes down, I'm practically useless unless my adrenaline is high.

Except I don't want to work right now. I want to continue to lay in Jake's arms.

I adjust against the mattress so I can roll to my back. Jake sighs but still naps. If I had any hope of sleeping at night I shouldn't keep resting, but he works nights often. Maybe his internal clock prefers to be awake during the later hours of the day—no matter his inability to sleep in.

There's a boyish quality to him with him relaxed this way. Resting against his slightly freckled skin are thick, dark eyelashes. They're darker than the rest of his hair, with the scruff on his jaw being the lightest of all.

His broad shoulder fills out the cap of his t-shirt, and where his arm extends past the sleeve hem, there's definition in his muscles, even at rest. I once again slip my fingers against his, this time so our fingers cross, resting our paired hands over my stomach. I won't sleep again, but I close my eyes to take in the moment.

Eventually, Jake takes a deep breath and his fingers flex against mine. Opening my eyes, I roll my head on my pillow to look at him. His eyes, now open, are heavy from his nap.

"Sleep okay?" I ask.

"Best damn nap," he answers groggily, closing his eyes once more. "Just give me a couple more minutes."

Upon unlacing our fingers, Jake groans his displeasure, his brows furrowing slightly. I can't help but grin as I roll to face him. I realize he's actually awake and just fighting against opening his eyes when the hand he keeps on me slips to my back and pulls me closer. I snuggle up to his warm body willingly, and when he lifts his knee, I slip my lower leg into the space. He drops his knee, locking my leg in place, and buries his nose into the crown of my head.

"You really do like to cuddle," I tease lightly.

"Mmm. You smell good. I smell you all over the damn room." His voice is still thick with sleep.

I've never had this.

I've never spent intimate moments just *being* with another person.

I had a long-term boyfriend in college, but our sleep-overs were far and few between. I always had early classes and he had late games.

I think I rather enjoy this…

No, I know I enjoy it.

Maybe too much.

"I know I have to go home," he continues, slowly and sleepily, although it's becoming more and more evident he's waking up. "Ben knows to feed and walk Boo, but I'm her person." He sighs heavily. "But fuck, I could do this all night."

"You can handle a few hours away from me," I tease. His answer is to pull me impossibly closer, and the sound that comes from him is a cross between a groan and a whine, and it makes me laugh.

It shouldn't be like this.

Not this quickly.

I feel like I'm getting in way over my head. Why do I attach to people so easily? What is it about Jake that makes me feel so dang comfortable, even though I barely know the man?

"Jake?"

"Hmm?"

I pull my head back and watch his face until he opens his eyes.

"I enjoyed myself today. Thank you."

"I did, too."

"Even though we didn't do anything more than hang out and then cuddle?"

"Best first date." He closes his eyes again and an amorous feeling floats through me.

"First date, 'ey?"

"You opposed to that?"

I shake my head against the pillow, my lips pressed together as I stare at him. Finally, I answer, "Not opposed at all."

We lay wrapped in one another for a little while longer before it's my turn to sigh. "I'm going to fall back to sleep if we stay here."

"Yeah. And I have to pee. So I guess that's our cue."

Untangling, we roll to opposite sides of the bed. Jake walks into the attached bathroom, closing the door, and I try to busy myself instead of listening to him because that's weird. After the pillows are back where they belong—I can't deal with clutter—I redo my ponytail and wait by my bedroom door.

He washes his hands—a point in his favor—and the door swings back open. Together, we walk downstairs.

Emina returned at some point and is sitting at the kitchen counter, eating from a Styrofoam container. She glances at the two of us, raises her brows, and pops a piece of sausage in her mouth.

It's probably ćevapi (*chae-vahp-ee*) from the Bosnian store.

I bet she has pita in that container too.

I wonder if she'd share...

"Good meeting?" Jake cuts through the silence, and Emina nods.

"The best. Good...afternoon?"

Jake chuckles and in a light tone, repeats her words. "The best." It's clear to me he's teasing, and not being suggestive.

For being muscles and scruff and chiseled jaw, Jake is far lighter—more carefree and fun—than I'd peg a guy like him for. He keeps surprising me at every turn.

Granted, it's only been one full day together. I still have a healthy amount of skepticism but I realize I *want* him to be this person.

I don't want to learn that this is all an act.

A show.

"I'm just going to walk him to the door. Save me some pita."

Emina closes the Styrofoam container and pulls it closer to her body, lowering her brows suspiciously. "How do you know I have pita? Maybe I just have ćevapi. Or maybe I have breakfast sausage and French toast from Mama Jo's."

Mama Jo's is a mom-and-pop diner that serves the best all-day breakfast. However, their takeout containers are those funky brown paper boxes that have four sides you pull down to secure.

"Because that's Styrofoam and the only place you grab takeout from with white Styrofoam is the Bosnian store."

She rolls her eyes good-naturedly, picks up a ćevapi, and points the sausage at me. "Go do what you have to do. I got you a plain cheese pita because you're a child who doesn't like spinach."

"Love you," I grin over my shoulder as Jake and I descend the stairs to the front door.

"I'm aware," she answers, and I don't need to look to know she rolls her eyes as she smiles.

Jake and I step out onto the front concrete slab and I close the door quietly behind us.

"I enjoyed today," I repeat, my voice soft as I look up. "Thank you."

"I did too." He reaches both hands to my hips, pulling me close. I respond by slipping my hands between his sides and arms, wrapping myself around him. Lifting my chin, he lowers his and we kiss for the first time today.

I can't explain the way I feel when I'm in Jake's arms. His kiss is powerful, yet he doesn't ask for more than I give.

Even though his arms are around me, there's nothing possessive...*aggressive* about his hold.

We're just two people in a close embrace, sharing a good —a really freaking good—kiss.

I lick my lips when I pull away, rolling them between my teeth after. Still, fear kicks in.

"You promise you're okay with taking things slow?"

Jake presses his lips to my forehead and I expect him to step away after, but he doesn't. I remain secure in his arms. "Promise. Listen." His voice is soft. "I have two sisters."

"Chandler and Hollis."

"Right. I'm protective as hell with them, and I know guys aren't always the most patient with women. If either of them told me they were pressured to go further with a guy than they were ready for, I'd find the asshole and teach him a lesson in respect. I can't be like that for them, but then not be the same type of guy I want for them."

"Even if you guys are miles and miles apart, they're lucky to have you as a brother."

"I like to think so." His cocky grin and wink tell me he's once again teasing, and I can't stop my smile from widening.

"I like you a lot, Jake. What's your last name?" I tip my head to the side.

"Wesley. Jake Wesley."

"Was that a dig at my anti-James Bond moment earlier?"

He chuckles, shaking his head, "Not at all. Swear it."

"Okay. Well, I like you a lot, Jake Wesley."

"Good. I like you a lot too, Sophia..."

"Burns."

"Sophia Burns."

Jake drops his head to kiss my lips once more, but this one remains G-rated.

Although he does suck my lower lip after, in a move that has my girly bits ready to say *"Fuck it. Fuck my standards. Fuck what I said earlier about slow. Fuck me."*

I can't stop the small moan from escaping my lips but he doesn't draw attention to it.

That is, until he presses a kiss to my cheek...my cheek bone...just in front of my ear...

And whispers, "When you play with yourself later, beautiful...think of me."

Eyes wide, face undoubtedly red, I pull my upper body back—my arms refuse to let go of their hold of the man, though. I'm not able to stay far for long before he has my chest pressed to his again.

"You saw it." I don't need to spell it out. The feel of my vibrator under my pillow comes back to mind in full force. Hell, the memory damn near has flashing neon signs.

His chuckle is short as his arms tighten slightly around me, but it's the puff of breath against my sensitive ear, then the way he takes a moment to suck the shell, that has me extremely aware of this man.

"I did," he doesn't bother denying. But then he does one better and admits, "I saw it the night I rescued you, too."

"Oh my god. That's so embarrassing." I close my eyes,

my arms finally loosening. When they start to fall, Jake's hands find mine and he locks our fingers together.

"Nothing to be embarrassed about. But maybe someday we can play with it together."

Narrowing my eyes, I regard him. "You'd play with sex toys?" My embarrassment is short-lived. *Curiosity wins every time with Sophia Burns.*

"Fuck, yes." He squeezes my hands before letting them go.

My mind goes wild at the possibilities. "Shoot, I might just ask you to sleepover tonight."

Jake's laughter is booming, and he throws an arm around my neck, and I'm once again in a close Jake embrace. This time, his erection is back and noticeable, and goodness, do I want to rub against him. Pull his cock out. Drop to my knees and put him in my mouth...

Instead, I take a deep breath from his shirt, enjoying the way he smells. It will have to do for now.

"Soph, I'm in for the long game," he says, still grinning. "Besides, waiting is part of the foreplay." He drops a kiss on the top of my head before taking a step back. "Good night, Sophia."

"G-good night, Jake."

He takes two steps away, walking backward, before turning.

One step.

Second step.

Third.

He's at the gate when I get the nerve to call out to him. "Will you think of me when you take care of... You know." I drop my eyes to where his sweatpants show his arousal. He doesn't even seem to care.

Jake pulls open the gate and turns his body back toward

me, but closes it between us before answering. "Better believe it. Your hands. Your mouth." Then his eyes drop and I know he's looking at where my legs meet.

Swallowing, I nod a few times, and finally admit, "I thought of you last night."

"And tonight?"

"I will tonight, too."

ELEVEN

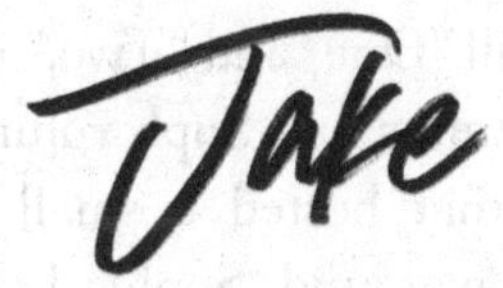

TWO WEEKS OF LEARNING SOPHIA.

They've been the best two weeks of my life, even if it's the most action my hand and cock have had together since high school.

There have been a lot of day dates.

Lunch dates.

Staying in dates and a couple going out ones, although before we went on the first she shared she sometimes gets overwhelmed when places are too loud and busy. One night that I didn't work, we went downtown to watch Matt Rife. She'd been laughing and enjoying the show while in the club but became extremely quiet on the ride home. Didn't bother me. She still smiled softly when I put my hand on her leg and offered answers to getting-to-know-you-better questions.

This lead to an accidental sleepover, where we fell

asleep in her bed while watching the week's episode of Ghosts.

She's met the zoo at mine and Ben's house and I wasn't surprised in the least that every single one of the Monsters, Inc. Crew loved her. In a move that did surprise me, Emina adopted the Things a few days ago.

Their names are Jedan (*yeh-dahn*) and Dva (*dvyeh*). When I told Emina they were cool names, she laughed and told me they were still "One" and "Two," just in Bosnian.

Last weekend, Emina and Soph volunteered for a local elementary school that hosted a small carnival to raise money for a new playground. Sophia helped bring awareness to the carnival in the days leading up to it, and on the day of, the pair was the "official" photographer and videographer. The images and videos they took and shared were instantly popular and had families discussing making the event an annual one.

Wanting to see Sophia work, I'd tagged along...and wasn't surprised in the least watching her interactions with the kids. She was good with the families, too, but she had a knack for getting a child to smile and twirl and gush about a prize they won playing one of the many carnival games.

She was especially good with the quieter children. The ones who watched from the outside, afraid to step in and participate.

In a few short weeks, I've seen many sides to Sophia and I like them all.

Today is one of my mid-shifts at O'Gallaghers, where I don't open but don't close, either. I'm looking forward to clocking out and hanging with Soph for a little bit later tonight.

She and Emina had a second meeting this afternoon with a couple who's getting married in Bali in a few short weeks. When Sophia first brought it up, I was excited for her—even when she expressed more than once how she wasn't worthy of being paid for that kind of service. She may feel like her best work is in editing but I've seen what she can do on the front end of filming, and an all-expenses paid trip to Bali to allow her to stretch her creative wings...? I'm all for it.

The one drawback, if you will, is the destination elopement means our first chunk of time apart is coming up and I'm not entirely looking forward to it.

Until then, I'm taking every moment I can get.

Including texting during my thirty-minute break.

ME:

What are you up to

I put my phone aside on the desk and take a bite of the grilled sandwich I asked tonight's cook, Chris, to make. Next week's schedule is attached to a clipboard and I pull it near, looking the single-week paper over. I should leave a note for Conor saying I can pick up extra hours in two weeks when the girls go on their trip. Take some time off before and after...

Get as much time with Sophia as I can before she leaves, and then keep myself busy while she's gone.

My phone starts to move against the desk as it vibrates. Flipping the device over, I see it's Sophia calling.

"Hey," I say into the phone. "How'd your meeting go?"

"Great!" Her smile is evident in her voice. "We went over their list of wants and needs, then Emina and I made a game plan. I've honestly never been so excited."

"I can hear it. What an amazing opportunity." I push the plate with the half-eaten sandwich away and lean back into the high-back leather seat. "You contacted your families?"

"I did. Just now, actually. Sent them emails with my plans and deadlines. I don't think the trip itself will affect much, honestly, but I wanted to be completely open with them. I'm a little nervous with two long flights but we'll be flying premium, which should be plenty of room for me to work on my regular laptop."

"You guys got your flights in order then?"

"We did. We'll leave Wednesday and land in Bali in the middle of the night, early Friday. Then leave super, super early on Monday, to arrive back in San Diego about dinner time. It'll be a thirty-two-hour Monday." Her groan makes me chuckle.

"Do you guys get a chance to explore? On Sunday?"

"Explore, or spend a day in an infinity pool that over-looks the forest or ocean. Something like that," she laughs.

"You sure you want to go with your best friend and not with, maybe, I don't know, me?" I tease, getting the second round of laughter I was aiming for. "Could definitely put an infinity pool to good use."

"Maybe if the flights don't dissuade me too much, you and I can do something fun and exotic some other time."

"Deal." The grin on my face is permanent when I talk to her. She has a way of keeping me light.

"When do you clock out? Eight, you said?"

"Yeah, eight. I have about ten minutes left of my thirty."

"Is it busy tonight?"

"Eh, not too terribly. A typical Wednesday night."

"Want me to meet you there? Then maybe we can grab food or something?"

"Or I can meet you at your place."

"That too…" For the first time since our call started, the cadence in her voice takes a dip.

If she wants to come out that badly, then I'm more than happy for her company. "I drove today," I say before pausing. "Maybe Emina can drive you here."

"I could walk. The sun won't set until seven or so."

It's not that *I* don't want her walking after dark. It's more she doesn't like to walk after the sun goes down. At least, not alone. "Do you really want to sit here for over an hour?"

"If you don't want me to—"

"Sophia, that wasn't the question, babe. Because I was literally just looking at the schedule and figuring out if Conor would let me take time off before you leave, and then work an asinine number of hours when you *are* gone because I won't know what the hell to do with myself. If you say you want to be here, I want you to be here. I'll make sure there's a spot at the bar for you."

"I thought it was a pub," she teases.

"No, *O'Gallaghers* is a pub," I grin. "The counter you *sit at* is a bar."

"Okay," Sophia chuckles lightly before getting back on topic. "Yes. I'd like that. And then we can walk to that new bakery before heading home."

Ah, so it's not dinner she's after, but a chance to scope out Lulu's down the street.

Anticipating the end of my day, I sit up in the chair again. "What time do you think you'll be here?"

"Maybe six-thirty?"

"Sounds good. I'll see you then."

We say our goodbyes and I quickly finish what remains of my sandwich.

IT'S SEVEN FORTY-FIVE.

The last fifteen minutes of this shift can't go by quick enough.

I saved a seat for Sophia by putting a glass of Sprite in a vacant spot after a patron left. The pace picked up right before she walked in, so I didn't get much time to talk with her but she didn't seem to mind. She nursed her drink, occasionally playing with the small, red cocktail straw, as she watched basketball on the television screen.

I'm wiping down the bar when she catches my attention. Crooking her finger, Sophia summons me over.

"What's up, beautiful?"

She leans into the bar and keeps her voice low. "Is that Trace Travers?" She tips her head sideways to point in the direction she wants me to look.

Glancing over, I see the hockey defenseman talking with Shayne, who will be clocking in for the late closing shift when I leave.

Nodding, I grin at my sport-loving girlfriend. "It is. You want an introduction?"

"I mean, I knew the Enforcers came here but I've never seen one out in the wild..."

"If he's here when I clock out, I'll introduce you to him. He's a good guy. They all are."

As I finish my shift, I keep an eye on Soph, who looks like a kid who was just told she's going to Disneyland.

That said, even if Shayne and Trace didn't have a thing going, I wouldn't be the least bit concerned about Sophia leaving me for him, regardless of how excited she is right now.

I do, however, pop over by the pair, and ask if Trace will stick around for a little bit so my girl can meet him.

At eight on the dot, I switch with Shayne, clocking out and walking to where Sophia sits. She slips off the chair and lays a ten dollar bill on the bar.

When I open my mouth, she holds up her hand. "Don't."

I roll my eyes, making Soph laugh, before leaning down to take the kiss I've wanted since she first walked in and sat at the bar. It's not that she's wearing anything overly sexy, just linen shorts with a long-sleeve shirt with "Are you for reel?" over the chest, an old-school film reel twisting through the words.

It's just...

Sophia.

And I always want my hands on her.

"I see you waited until I was off the clock," I joke between pecking her lips twice.

Sophia's mouth curls against mine as she taps my chest with the flat of her hand. "Because you would have put it in your pocket and given it back to me later. I've got your number. I don't care if it doesn't go toward my soda because you're silly and covered it, but it can go to the night's tip pool."

There's someone waiting for her seat, so I put my arm around her shoulders and usher Sophia out of the way. With just enough room to walk side by side, I take the opportunity to keep her in my arms as I maneuver her toward the end of the bar where Trace Travers still sits.

When she realizes we're not going for the door, Sophia's footsteps slow. "Jake..."

"He's a nice guy, Soph. Meet him. I know damn near every person on their roster—and their wives and kids. Get this one out of the way so it's easier later." Because if she and I stay together for the long haul, she'll be meeting everyone eventually.

Whether it's here or during functions.

Conor's close with the coach, and more often than not, an O'Gallagher family and pub "team" function includes a pop in or two from the Prescotts, at minimum.

We're a few feet away when she whispers, "I'm nervous!"

Grinning, I drop my arm from her shoulders but only so I can hold her hand. "Don't be. He's honestly a regular dude."

"But he's a three-time Conn Smythe trophy winner. That means he's been voted, *thrice*," I have to hold back my chuckle, "to be the MVP of his team during playoffs. AND! He was nominated for the Willie O'Ree Community Hero Award last year, after starting a youth-hockey group for kids living on base in Hawaii."

"Maybe don't spout his stats and achievements when you meet him," I joke, even though I'm sure he wouldn't mind.

Sophia isn't the first fan he's encountered.

She won't be the last, either.

Catching movement, Trace glances at us as we near. He stands from his stool, although clearly not giving up his spot, and holds out a hand. "Jake."

"Trace." Keeping a hand in Sophia's, Trace and I greet eachother with a pull-in-back-tap handshake every guy on the team seems to do. "This is Sophia. She's a big fan."

Sophia, far calmer than I figured she'd be after the information she rattled off just moments before, smiles and extends her own hand. "Hi, Trace."

Trace gives her hand a squeeze. "It's nice to meet you, Sophia."

We stand and talk for a bit. In the last few weeks, I've learned about Sophia's history of playing hockey and lacrosse, but she's more animated about it now while discussing it with him. They talk about growing up playing a competitive sport, and I learn that while Trace's dad was stationed in Honolulu during his tenure with the Navy, he had to give up the sport for a season—before he went back stateside, living with an aunt and uncle so he could continue to play.

Sophia's comment about him starting a hockey club in Hawaii makes sense now.

I love watching the way she talks when she's passionate about something. Her face lights up and she has some state of smile on her face the entire time.

I know I won't be the one to stop their conversation based on her joy alone, and thankfully, I don't have to.

Sophia's smile widens one more time before she waves a hand between the three of us. "Well, thank you for letting me talk your ear off. We need to head out if we're going to catch Lulu's before they close for the night."

"It was nice to meet you, Sophia. Good seeing you, Jake," Trace grins as he sits back down on the stool.

"Gosh, this has been the best day ever," Sophia muses happily once we're outside on the sidewalk. "It's like the universe is smiling down on me."

A lesser man would take offense to the comment, thinking that maybe his girl has a crush on the hot athlete, but I've gotten to know Sophia enough to know...she's just had a really good day.

"Well, I'm about to make it better," I chuckle.

"Oh, how I hope they have things available and haven't

started closing up for the night. Wouldn't that be the pits? We walk there and they only have like...two measly cookies? Although, I'm sure they'd be delicious measly cookies."

This time, I laugh. "You're always a few steps ahead, aren't you?"

"Gotta be prepared."

"Positive thoughts, babe. I'm sure they'll have plenty for you to choose from."

And they do.

Not only do they have five different types of cookies, but they also have a few cupcakes, two log cakes, brownies, and fudge.

So much for my earlier thought that Sophia was like a kid who was told she was going to Disneyland.

The correct place would have been Lulu's.

We leave with two pounds of fudge—one in milk chocolate and the other a dark chocolate peanut butter—one of each cookie, and after a lot of debating, one s'mores cupcake that we'll split.

"Are we going to hang out at your place or mine?" Sophia asks, buckling into the passenger seat once we're at O'Gallaghers and in the back lot. The O'Gallagher siblings keep this lot available for staff only, so when other trucks come by— not just the food and drink suppliers, but repair men and the like—they have a way to access the building quickly. "With Ben closing, probably yours I'm guessing, for the animals."

"Do you mind?" I put the truck in reverse, and maneuver out of the parking spot.

"Not at all. Can we run by my house too? I have something for them."

It doesn't take long before we're at the complex and Sophia's hopping back in my truck with a canvas bag in her lap. When I reach over to look inside, she grins and slaps my hand away.

"It's a surprise!"

"I thought it was for the animals?" I laugh, driving to the opposite end of the complex.

When we get to mine and Ben's unit, Boo is waiting patiently at the door but the moment she spots Sophia, her butt begins her happy wiggling until she's practically in a shaking, tippy-toe dancing, C-shape.

Sophia bends and gives her all the love she asks for, accepting the weight as Boo leans happily into her legs.

"Let me feed the cats then we can take Boo for a quick walk," I suggest, squeezing past Sophia's upturned ass. I fight like hell to not focus on her bent in half.

I've been the model "we're going slow" boyfriend.

Even during those massive makeout sessions we have, I keep my hands to myself.

Or on her shoulders...her back...her neck and face...

But nothing that will move us to the next base.

I've wanted nothing more than to feel the weight of her breasts in my hands. To run my thumbs over her erect nipples that fight against her shirt, whenever kissing goes from sweet and innocent, to hot and indecent.

To slip my hand over the curve of her ass, sinking my fingertips where her thighs meet her core...

On the flip side, I feel like we're building a solid base. I haven't felt this connected to a woman...

Ever.

Sophia hands me the paper bag from Lulu's to bring into the kitchen as she places her canvas tote at her feet.

"Want me to bring that in, too?" I point to the bag.

"I don't trust you not to peek," she teases, standing up to

grab Boo's connected leash and harness from it's home on a hook designed as a dog's backend.

"Something tells me—"

She cuts me off. "No peeking! I mean it. The gang will be sad when I take my bag and go home without giving them any of their surprises."

With an exaggerated sigh, I tell her, "Fine."

Her smile bright, Sophia leans in to kiss my cheek. "Good. I'll take her potty in the yard so she doesn't derail the feeding, and then we can take her for a walk."

TWELVE

AFTER DISCUSSING IT WITH EMINA—BECAUSE what else are best friends good for?—I decided tonight was the night.

Tonight's the night I give in to the desire that races through my body anytime Jake so much as *looks* in my direction.

And I brought all the good things to make sure we're able to have uninterrupted time together.

I wouldn't put it past Boo to watch the entire time, or for Mike to take residence on the pillow next to my head, purring in my ear from start to finish.

No thanks.

Not while I'm being railed by the man who's starred in every sexual fantasy I've had in the last month.

Their attention will be focused elsewhere for a little while tonight, thank you very much.

In the time I've known Jake, we've spent more hours

together than I have with any human besides my family or Emina. I feel more myself when I'm *with* him than when I'm alone. It's as if he brings out qualities that have lain dormant for years and I'm starting to recognize myself again.

Like Emina said all those weeks ago: he lights me up.

He doesn't get annoyed when I suggest we stay in and he doesn't pester when I get quiet after hours of being "on" and social.

Hell, not only does he respect my occasional need for low-key, he's been the one to suggest it at times.

It may have only been a few weeks but I'm confident that sleeping with Jake won't change anything. There's not a niggling thought, not a devil on my shoulder, that attempts to convince me otherwise—and I've spent a lot of the last ten years listening to those narratives.

I feel nothing but good and secure about my decision.

The top of my canvas bag folds over on itself and as much as I know Jake is clearly aware there's more going on in that bag than a few treats and toys for the animals, I trust he won't look.

With Boo's harness in place, I take her out into the small yard and she immediately does her business. She's a good girl like that. I've noticed on walks that she won't potty in other yards or even at the park. Boo prefers to keep things at home, and I don't blame her.

Regardless of his dog's potty habits, Jake is a responsible owner and has a poop bag holder connected to the leash. The added bone-shaped dispenser is pink, and I can't decide if it's because Boo's a girl or if it's because of the animated character she's named for.

Jake comes out of the townhouse at the same time Boo

starts kicking back grass with her hind legs. "You two ready?"

"We are. She just finished up."

After stepping out of the yard, he holds out his hand. "Want me to take her?"

"Nah. I've got her."

Instead of taking the leash, he opts to take my hand. We talk about my upcoming trip with Emina as we walk leisurely around the complex, the dark night lit by numerous lights around the parking lot and sidewalks, and when Boo starts to pick up her pace as we near the community's dog park, we decide to let her get some sniffing in and allow her to lead the way. The community rules state the park is closed after sundown but we open and shut the double gates quietly. It's not like Boo will make a ruckus by herself. She just sniffs happily along the fencing, grass, and the random bushes in the rock bed border.

She enjoys her off-leash sniffing time although she never leaves her mark.

"She's too good to leave a response to her pee-mails," I joke quietly.

When she's through, she sits by the gate and looks over at us.

We make it back to Jake's a solid thirty minutes after leaving.

"Can I look in the bag now?"

Grinning, I hand him the leash and harness. "Nope. Not yet."

"I'm hearing that I *will* be able to look."

"You would be right."

Instead of putting the bag over my shoulder, I grasp the top in my fist as we move into the living area. Sully is taking a nap on the cat tower but Mike greets us by slinking between Jake's legs and then mine.

I squat to pick up the gray feline. The moment I do, he stretches his long, hefty, tom-cat body so his front legs are extended over my shoulder and he's held like a child on the hip. "Let's see what I've got for you all."

At the kitchen peninsula, I put the bag down and let the top fall open. It doesn't reveal all, which only serves to tease Jake a little longer. "You just sit over there," I direct, nodding to one of the stools on the opposite side. With a crooked smirk, he does—after attempting to pull himself taller to look inside from where he stands.

Reaching in, first I pull out a rubber ball that isn't smooth like a normal ball. "This is called a Wunderball." I reach out over the counter to hand it to Jake to remove the cellophane wrapping. "It's supposed to be indestructible and good for her teeth, because of all the grooving. It says it's all-natural, too."

"Someone really sold you over, didn't they?" Jake jokes, bringing the ball to his teeth to puncture a hole in the wrap.

"I also read reviews, and owners with dogs who destroy all the things said this was a good deal. They come in all sorts of colors and if she likes that one, I'll grab some of the others, too."

Jake shakes his head with a grin as he pulls apart from where he broke open the packaging, releasing the ball. Boo sits impatiently at his side, her tail wagging in quick move-ments. Instead of handing it to her though, Jake lets it bounce on the wood-style linoleum.

The ball doesn't bounce straight up and down. Because of the grooves, it ends up bouncing in a zigzag pattern, causing Boo to pounce in the wrong direction more than once.

Her excitement wakes Sully from his nap. With a mew upon landing, he hops off the tree and comes to investigate. I have cat-nip mice and crinkle balls for the felines of the house, and soon, every one of the Monsters, Inc. Crew is happily playing.

"Do I get to look in the bag now?" Jake asks as I pull out boxes of treats—one large tub of freeze-dried liver treats for the cats, and two smaller containers for Boo, one of which contains a treat called Papa Psuka.

Ignoring his question for the moment, I explain the last one. "This here is beef lung, and the cats can have it too, if you want to break it apart. They had samples in the store—"

"Did you try one?" Jake teases.

I fake-gag. "No. They smell terrible. But again, I was told dogs love them. As for the cats, if you want to break them apart, you can, but personally, I'd handle them as infrequently as possible. I could smell them in my car and they're in a sealed container!"

He grabs the sealed plastic tub and looks at the label. "Where'd you find all this stuff again?"

"Bella's Barkery. It's a boutique pet store I found the other day." Jake lifts his brows at 'boutique' and I shrug. "It was a really cute store. And you'd get bored with the same ol' cookies every day, too, so it's okay to treat with fun cookies now and again."

"I can tell you about a cookie I wouldn't get bored of..."

A stupid grin on my face, I push the bag at him. "You haven't sampled this cookie yet, so you can't say that for sure."

"I can assure you, I wouldn't bore of what you gave," he teases right back, sliding the bag closer to him. He looks inside...

When he looks back up, it's him who has a stupid-silly grin on his face, brows up in question.

"So. How about I let you try that sample?" Surprisingly, the words that leave my mouth have me feeling equal parts excitement and nerves. Not once in the hours since Emina and I talked have I felt nervous for this moment, but here I am.

"It's on the tip of my tongue to ask if you're sure, but you'd probably call that a questionable red flag—" he jokes from one of our earlier conversations "—so I'm going to assume you've thought this out and I'm not going to look a gift horse in the mouth."

He stands from the stool, grabbing the bag with one hand and crooking two fingers in my direction in a come hither manner. As I step around the counter, he holds that same arm out so I can take his hand.

"An intentional sleepover tonight?" he asks.

"I mean... I *did* come over after nine at night." Resorting to banter is easier.

"True, but you brought sleep clothes. Or tomorrow clothes."

"Sleep clothes," I clarify, my head picturing the shorts and tank that are at the bottom of the bag.

Under my bright pink vibrator.

"Hmm," is his only answer. At least, until we reach his room. "I should put Boo in her crate for the night," he says, but instead, closes his bedroom door.

He tosses the bag and it lands at the end of the bed at the same time he releases my hand and grabs my hips, twisting me to face him.

"She'll be fine. She's preoccupied." I slid my hands up his chest until they link behind his neck.

Jake lowers his head and then we're kissing, the animals

forgotten. His mouth on mine, his tongue refamiliarizing itself in my mouth, he walks me backward until my legs hit the mattress. Both of his hands move to cup my ass but only long enough for him to lift me.

I gasp against his mouth, but the sound melts into a moan as he lays me back, pressing my body into the bed with his weight. I can feel the long column of his cock behind his pants and I'm more than excited to finally move our relationship to the next level.

I'm ready to feel him moving in me, his body surrounding me, his muscles flexing over me.

Weeks of foreplay tell me Jake won't be a selfish lover in bed.

And if I'm wrong?

Well, I'll cross that bridge if I come to it.

He slips his hand under my shirt and my stomach concaves at the touch. With lazy brushes, his thumb rubs back and forth as my body relaxes under him again, although "relax" is relative.

My panties are nearly uncomfortable with how wet I am, anticipating what comes next. My nipples are tight and my chest aches as I think about his mouth on them.

My body is so primed and ready, it won't take long for me to come.

Quick regret that tonight will be over sooner than he's probably used to flashes in my mind.

Jake trails his kisses toward my ear and licks the lobe into his mouth before whispering, "I want to see how you play with yourself." He glides his hand up my skin to cup my lace-covered breast—I made sure to wear my good panties set. Between his hand and the way he sucked on my ear, my nipples are tight and aching for stimulation. "Fuck, I want to be the one to make you come but damn, Soph, I've done nothing but think about you and that fucking magenta dick."

He moves his kiss to my neck and I tip my head to the side, sighing when he licks a spot before nibbling gently. "It's usually fast," I whisper on a moan. "Not worth a show."

"Watching you come apart is definitely worth the show," he replies, pushing back to kneel between my splayed legs. He trails his hands down the tops of my thighs, to my knees, and then back up again, this time gliding over my inner thighs. I roll my hips against the bed, pushing my head back into the pillow. The need coursing through me is strong.

When his fingers slip under the legs of my shorts but stop before they can meet wet lace, a whimper leaves my lips.

"Do you touch yourself first?" he asks, sliding both hands so he cups the tops of my thighs, yet keeping his thumbs near my core. He's so close to touching me and hell, if he'd just swipe up a little bit...

I'm so freaking wet, I know I'd easily be able to push my vibrator in if I wanted—and I usually can't get to this level of relaxed by myself.

I don't ever recall getting this far, this fast. Not with Josh. Not with Nate in college.

"Do you work yourself up with your hand before you use your vibrator? Do you roll your hips against the dick head, looking for release, or do you fuck yourself while pinching your nipples? Tell me, Soph, how do you get off every night?" I tip my hips, trying to get him to brush a thumb over my center, but he pulls his hands away instead. "I can smell how turned on you are, Sophia. Show me."

Swallowing, I nod against the pillows. "O-okay."

His grin is damn near wicked as he leans back in his

kneel, reaching for the discarded bag and pulling out my toy. "No lube?" he asks after looking inside and seemingly moving what I use for pajamas aside.

"I don't usually insert," I tell him, and I can feel myself blushing from chest to cheeks. The vibrator is pretty realistic in size but I can never relax fully to loosen up enough for the hard silicone to feel pleasant.

Not a problem tonight, I'm sure.

"Interesting." He holds the toy out and I take it.

"I'm usually in my pajamas..."

His hands are on my thighs again. "I'd say put them on for the full experience, but they'll just get in the way." The way he looks at me, the absolute hunger in his expression, gives me all the confidence I need to continue.

I place the vibrator on the bed beside me and arch my back, working my shirt up and off. Jake holds his hand out and I give him the garment, although all he does with it is toss it toward the wall.

"May I?" His fingers rub the lower hem of my shorts.

"Yes."

I lift my legs from the bed as he removes my shorts and those too get tossed at the wall. Left in a pretty lace bra and thong set from Victoria's Secret, I keep my eyes on his face as I put a hand on my stomach. "First I touch myself like this," I tell him, dragging my nails up and down over my stomach softly. Goosebumps always eventually occur, but they happen immediately tonight.

No doubt because I have an enraptured audience of one.

Whispering, I dictate what happens next. "When it starts to feel like my nipples are tight, I'm ready for the next bit." His eyes drop from my face to my chest and I unclip the front clasp of my bra. I release only my left boob and start to drag a nail around my nipple, close but not touching. "This one always feels better."

"Noted." His voice is lower and more gravelly than normal, and that tone alone could make me come. His turned-on, sex voice does it for me.

I continue to watch him as I draw light circles around and around, until finally dragging my nail over the tight peak.

Not hard.

A whisper of a touch.

It makes my breath catch.

I flick my nipple a few times before I begin to roll it between my finger and thumb, sometimes brushing my thumb over the top, sometimes squeezing harder only to go back to the super light, featherlike touches.

Even though the other isn't nearly as sensitive, I pull the lace from the covered breast and roll that nipple too, until I'm more than ready to turn my vibrator on.

"I usually just move my shorts to the side," I explain. "But..." Instead of what is typical, I start to push my lacy thong down, and like before, Jake is happy to assist in taking them off.

Should I feel weird explaining how I get myself off? Because I don't. If anything, it feels incredibly erotic to be in this space with him. Lying in his bed with my bra half on and nothing else, my legs spread as he sits between them. The only thing that would make it better would be to feel his hands on my skin.

Knowing the buttons and settings by heart, I blindly grab the toy and turn it on. Once the mostly quiet sound of vibrating fills the room, I hit the uppermost button four times—normal vibe, harder vibe, hardest vibe, crescendo vibe—and place the realistically shaped, mushroomed head directly to my clit. I sigh and go back to gently rolling my left nipple.

Watching Jake watch me is a bigger turn-on than I'd ever expect. He can't decide where to pay the most attention—my pussy, my tits, or my face. Honestly, I'm surprised he doesn't keep his eyes on the wet flesh between my legs.

"Sometimes I like to use the head like this." I use just the very tip and slide it up and down my center, sometimes stopping at my entrance and giving it a little circle before going back up to my clit, circling there, too. God, I'm so close... "Usually I just place it here," I swallow the mouthful of saliva I have as my need grows, and angle the head so the bulk of it rests right on my clit, "and I imagine you pounding into me," I confess, lifting and lowering my hips, rolling them against the bed in slow waves, as I do just that. My eyes close and even though he's sitting right there, I allow my imagination to remove his clothes and put him over me, his fists beside my head as he drives his cock in and out of me. My hips begin moving quicker, which causes my clit to rub deliciously against the vibrating toy, and I know I'm going to come in three, two...

Just as I crest the top, pleasure rushing through my body, Jake pushes two fingers into me and I gasp anew at both my orgasm and the intrusion. I pull the vibrator away from my sensitive clit at the same time he crashes his mouth to mine. I'm still riding my high but feeling his fingers in me is prolonging my climax in a way I've never experienced. I whimper against his mouth as he finger fucks me through clenching muscles.

He milks my orgasm for all it's worth, twisting his hand in a way that allows him to rub what can only be my G-spot.

Unable to focus on breathing and pleasure, I pull my mouth away and gulp for air as he quickly works that secret spot. My knees draw up and my thighs tighten against his hard body as he leans over top of me, his lips now on my neck.

"Oh my god, oh my god, I'm... I'm..."

"Again," he demands...and I do.

I come again.

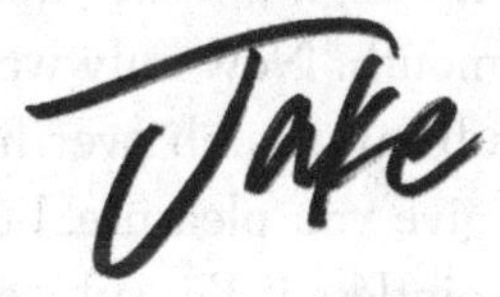

THIRTEEN

FUCKING.

Beautiful.

Sophia falling apart in my bed of her own accord was better than any fantasy I had, but then helping her into a second, immediate, orgasm...

I will be jacking off to this moment for years to come, I have little doubt.

Watching her pleasure herself has me harder than steel. I debated whether or not I was allowed to touch her, but trusted she wouldn't be here if she didn't want my hands on her.

As her body calms, I sit back on my knees to watch as I pull my fingers from her, anticipating the sight of her cum as I do. "You're so fucking soaked," I comment, a rope of her wetness coming with my hand. "I want to eat you out."

Her chest is still heaving although her breaths aren't as labored as a minute ago. "While I think that would be fun, I don't know that I have another orgasm in me and that would just make it pointless."

Chuckling, I lift my hand to my lips and suck off one finger. Not sure how dirty Soph can be, I bring the other finger, still wet with her, to her lips.

Our eyes lock and she opens her mouth.

"Fuck," I groan, enjoying far too much the way her tongue swipes over the digit and her lips tighten as I slide my finger from her mouth. Now only wet with her saliva, I cup her chin and rub my thumb over her lower lip. "Yes, eating you out is to give you pleasure, but trust me when I say, it wouldn't be pointless if I'm subjected to being down there for an hour before you come again."

"You wouldn't..."

I lift a single brow. "Is that a challenge?"

She opens her mouth and closes it. "Maybe not tonight," she finally settles on, suppressing laughter.

Winking, I say, "That's what I thought."

Perhaps I'm feeling a little too cocky though because Sophia surprises me when she manages to roll us, absolutely no mind to the fact she's leaving a wet spot on my shirt. "You may not be going down on me right now, but I can certainly go down on you..." She wiggles back until she sits on my upper thighs, her hands making quick work of my jeans and freeing my cock.

I'd rather be in her, but I haven't seen a woman as excited to suck dick as Soph is right in this moment, so I get comfortable and watch as she lowers her head.

I move to rest on my elbows, clearing my throat. "Just to put it out there—" Anticipation builds throughout my body but she doesn't touch her lips to me yet, "I don't expect this."

"Debating if that's a red flag or green one," she purrs

with a fleeting, sassy grin. Then the tip of her tongue is out and swiping at the drop of precum that weeps, and words are no longer available.

This I have to watch, I think as I crunch further up to sit.

With my cock in her fist, Sophia grins at me before pressing her lips to mine in a hard kiss, her hand starting to move up and down my shaft. As she works me, I work her mouth...until our tongues are dueling for dominance. When she pulls back from the kiss briefly to suck on my lower lip, I decide she wins this round.

I let her take complete control the next time our mouths meet.

I'd be happy with this, kissing and a hand job, but she's clearly on a mission. It's her that pulls from our heavy making out and instead of playing and licking, taking her time, she suddenly drops her mouth wide, taking my cock almost to the hilt.

"Shit, Soph," I groan, my fingers gripping into the sheets under me. I fight to not drop my head and close my eyes.

Gotta watch.

Releasing one hand from the bed, I cup her cheek before sliding my hand to the back of her head, but only so I can wrap her ponytail in my hand. "You look so good taking my cock. Your lips around me. Fuck, yes."

She hums and this time, I can't stop from dropping my head back momentarily to enjoy the sensation. Her head bobs as she moves up and down, and her breasts sway with each movement. I let go of her ponytail, giving in to the desire to tweak one of her tight nipples and I watch as every inch of her body tightens in a shudder of pleasure.

I continue to roll the tip between my fingers. I won't be coming in her mouth and I'll be damned if she's done getting hers tonight. I need to make sure she's primed for another orgasm.

Two is great.

Three is better.

When I realize I'm playing with the "wrong" nipple, I change the hand I lean back into so I can give proper attention to the one she says feels better. A very similar full-body shudder moves over her but this time, her breath hitches through her nose, too.

Ah. Yes. Better.

I squeeze a little harder and her moan lets me know she's enjoying it. She pops her mouth from my cock and presses her chest closer to my hand, pumping me in her fist faster and harder.

Now that she's not leaning into my lap, I sit up straighter and hook a hand around her neck, pulling her up for a kiss. Our mouths clash as she keeps working me, and I her.

Tonight is so much better than I could have ever imagined. We're in a sync I've never experienced and I know the moment she takes my cock into her wet, tight pussy, it will easily be the best sex I've had.

She's been worth the waiting. The biding of time until she was ready.

"Sit," I say against her mouth. Her lowered lids lift and those hazel orbs focus on my eyes. "Take my cock. I want to feel you around me. Riding me."

I'm half afraid she'll decide tonight's not the night after all, but I should know better.

When she releases her grip from my length, I can't stop the groan from passing my lips. She places both hands on my shoulders as she braces a knee on either side of my hips. Once she's secure on the bed, a hand releases my shoulder to once again grab my cock, but this time so she can line us up.

I frame her face with my hands, bringing her back to our previous activity. Except this time, our kisses aren't as frantic. Not as frenzied.

Her tongue brushes over mine as she sinks slowly, taking my cock inch by glorious inch. She doesn't take and pull back, take a little more and pull back...

She just sits and takes me.

Her pussy grips my cock tightly and hell if I don't nearly come right then and there. "Shit, you feel so good," I moan against her mouth, at the same time she says damn near the same thing.

She stops kissing me long enough to smile, a light laugh filling my ears before she whispers, "Jinx. You owe me—"

"An orgasm," I promise. "Ride my cock like the good girl you are."

The way she rolls her hips, taking me in and out of her body, sends my senses higher than I'd figure slow fucking could do. Her tits brush against my chest and, fucking A, I'm wearing too many clothes.

I have a fully naked Sophia in my arms, in my lap, *on my cock*, and I'm still fucking clothed from head to toe, except for my dick.

Holding her ass to keep her secure, I move to turn us, once again putting Soph on her back.

I like her there. I'd like to keep her right here, to continue thrusting into her heat, but I need my skin touching hers more.

I start to push away long enough to disrobe but Soph grabs a fistful of my shirt. "No," she moans. "I need... I want..." She hooks a leg around my ass in an attempt to keep me in place.

"You'll get. I promise." I kiss her chin. Her jaw. "But I want my skin on yours."

"Oh. That too." She doesn't release her leg from her hold though. Instead, she starts to bunch the fabric of my shirt, pulling it up to expose my stomach. Guess we're doing it this way.

I brace on one hand and bring the other to my upper back. Between her pushing the material up and me pulling it over my head, I get the shirt off and pooling around my braced arm before tossing it in the general direction of her clothes. When my chest is as bare as hers, she wraps her arms around my neck at the same time she pushes her tits into my chest.

"Yes. Better," she murmurs. She's rubbing her nipples against my chest, moaning at the sensation.

She's taken getting herself off into her own hands.

I grasp both her wrists and pin them beside her head on the pillow, flattening my chest to hers. "Your orgasm is mine," I growl and instead of moaning or whimpering, she smiles devilishly up at me.

"Do your best work," she taunts.

Her sassy smile falls off her face though when I take her left nipple into my mouth, playing and sucking with all my worth. Her pussy walls ripple around my cock in response.

After playing long enough to have her body writhing, I gently scrape my teeth over the sensitive peak before kneeling between her legs. I grasp her hips and pull her back so her ass rests on my knees, changing our angle. I'm restricted by my jeans hanging around my hips, but I'm too busy chasing an orgasm to care.

Soph places her feet on my shoulders, arching her back against the bed. "Oh, yes..."

I continue my slow, sensual thrusts into her in this position, enjoying the way her body flushes as she gets closer and closer to coming. Her head rolls from side to side and her breaths become erratic.

So fucking beautiful.

I wrap a hand around an ankle and turn my head to kiss the bone there, never expecting—

"*F-f-f-fu-u-ck.*" The word is shaky as her body convulses through an orgasm.

My cock is being squeezed so fucking hard. I let her legs drop to the bed and lean over her, her ass still in my lap, and drive into her quickly now, my cock pushing against her pulsing walls to extend her orgasm and to get my own.

"Yes. Fuck, yes. Like that. Yeah, Soph." I don't truly pay attention to the words as I say them, only that everything I'm feeling in the moment amounts to the best sex I've had.

I'm one second away from releasing my load into her when I realize in my haste to get in her, I never protected her. "Fuck," I groan, pulling out just in time to let ropes of cum coat her stomach. "Yes, shit. Yeah," I continue to grunt and groan, holding my cock in a tight fist. I give it another good tug but I'm wrung dry.

I collapse face-down on the bed next to her and we both take a moment to catch our breath.

"So yeah," Soph says into the otherwise quiet room some time later, rolling her head so she can look at me. I open my eyes to see her grinning at me. "My orgasm was yours like you said. Again. Better than I can give myself."

"Backatcha," I manage, exhausted. "That was..."

"Good?"

"Fucking phenomenal." But then a fear knocks on my mind. "It was just good for you?" She's still smiling. That has to be a positive sign, right?

"Jake?" She says my name instead of answering.

"Yeah?"

"You're still wearing your jeans. If it was—" she lifts a hand to air quote, "'just good' you would be fully naked. I'd have been all, yeah, sure, take off your pants. Your cock's good and all but, yeah, take it out and let's just start over. But no. I didn't say that."

I hear her lighthearted teasing and give it right back to her. "If you give me a couple minutes, I'll take 'em off and we can start over. Maybe it'll be fucking phenomenal for you next time."

She laughs, and I get the feeling I may never get enough of this woman.

And the thought doesn't scare me in the slightest.

———

WE SHOWER TOGETHER and when we're through washing—only to be primed for another round between the sheets—Sophia doesn't bother with the pajamas she brought.

She just slips into my bed like she belongs, as I walk into the living room to make sure Boo didn't destroy the place.

She didn't.

In fact, she took herself to bed.

At the sound of me walking into the living room, she looks up from where she's curled in her crate but doesn't move to get up, although her tail begins moving frantically in happiness. It's well past her bedtime and she has a fairly strict routine.

"Night, Boo," I tell her, closing the door and dropping the blanket that will envelop her completely in darkness, just as she likes. Even when Ben comes home in a couple of hours, she won't want to get up.

Making sure the place is secure for the night, I go back to my bedroom, closing the door and locking it for good measure.

The overhead light is off but Soph turned on the small nightstand lamp beside my bed and I can see she has her knees drawn up under the covers. Her smile is wicked and I swear I hear a buzzing.

I don't bother guessing; I know she has her vibrator between her legs. "How close are you?" I walk to the side of the bed she lays in and grab the comforter and sheet, pulling them back to expose her nude body, and my suspicions are confirmed.

"Not very close, unfortunately," she admits. "But if I squeeze my eyes shut and imagine you while clamping down on my pussy, I can probably get there." I'm not used to a woman being completely forthcoming with her thoughts when it comes to sex. It's a major turn-on.

I lean down to press a kiss to her knee. "You ever use it while getting fucked?" After running my tongue in a circle over her skin, I gently bite, scraping my teeth against the hard surface.

"You wanna be the first?" No second-guessing. No preamble.

Just... Honest.

"Fuck, yeah."

I pull a box of condoms out from my nightstand and quickly cover myself. I will be experiencing this round completely within the walls of her sex. She stretches her legs out as I move to put myself between her legs and when I reach for the vibrator that's against her pussy, she lets me take it.

Not without question, though. "I thought..."

"Can't have you coming too soon," I tell her. "Would

hate for you to just have to lay there while I pound mercilessly into you." I notch my cock at her entrance and push in slowly, enjoying each inch as she stretches around me.

Definitely a different feeling before, bare, but I'm in no way ready to procreate.

"Oh, heaven forbid that," she moans, lifting her hips and spreading her legs further to take me easier.

Even though I was just in her hardly thirty minutes ago, it's like her cunt sucked back into tight mode. I'm glad I didn't just plunge into her and instead opted for the delicacy of slow fucking.

Our bodies move against one another, her moans in my ear and my groans against her skin. There's time for fast and multiple positions. Right now, I'm enjoying this sensuous dance—and the growing slickness of her pussy tells me she is too.

I nearly forgot the entire purpose of what we're doing and come back online long enough to ask, "My fingers or your vibrator?" Gliding my hand down her body, I let my fingers move over her wet curls and press two digits against her engorged clit.

"Vibrator," she says with a breathless sigh, dragging a foot over the back of my calf. "Your hand's nice but I want to remember how your cock feels when I use it next time..."

Ideally, next time will also involve my cock, but I did tell her I wanted to play with her toy. So this time, we play.

I reach for the discarded vibrator, our bodies still connected as intimately as they can be, and press all three buttons before I find the one that turns the toy on.

"Hit the top button two more times," she instructs and I do. The vibing gets harder and louder.

Holding my hips against hers, my cock completely

sheathed by her, I move so I know I'm putting the head where she wants it.

The moment it makes contact though, she shrieks—although her pussy flutters wildly against me. "Oh. Okay, no."

I take it off as quickly as I placed it.

"I'll come way too fast," she explains. "Turn it off and on again. Just the lowest setting is good."

Grinning crookedly at her and her absolute unabashedness with fucking with her toy, I again do as she says. This time when I put it on her sensitive skin, she sighs.

"Oh yes. Yeah, that's good."

"You take it," I tell her. "I'm good at multitasking but..."

I have way too many other things I want to do to your body right now and won't be able to if I'm trying to make sure I hold this in place correctly.

Soph's hand brushes mine as she takes the toy and I reward her by sucking her tit into my mouth, my tongue playing over her nipple. I nibble and suck, bite and roll it between my teeth. Her breathing pattern tells me she's just about there again and that's good because I'm going to have to start counting to one hundred and back to make sure I don't get off before her.

"In your imagination, is it slow like this or rough?" I move to kiss between her breasts before giving the other nipple a fraction of the attention her "good" nipple got.

"This is nice," she moans in answer.

"Not the question, Soph. Not that intend for you to have to use your imagination but for your memories..." If I have my way, she'll mostly get off with me but I know we can't be together all the time. Hell, she's going out of the country in a few weeks.

God knows I have a ton of new memories to jerk off to. I want her to have the same.

"Ugh. Fine..." She uses her free hand to play with her left nipple as I continue to gently lap the other. "Fast."

I give her what she wants and later, during round three of the night, we try again with her on her stomach, and me taking her from behind. It would seem that position *really* gets her going.

Hell, the moment she was on her stomach, her ass in the air, and her vibrator between her legs, she was nearly flying off the handle.

We finally exhaust ourselves a few orgasms later, and not a moment too soon. After turning off the lamp and settling in for the rest of the night, I hear the front door open and shut as Ben comes home.

"Good timing," Sophia whispers, hearing it too.

Chuckling, I press a kiss to her cheek before pulling her to be my little spoon. "Good night, Soph."

"G'night, Jake."

FOURTEEN

WE SPEND the next ten days fucking.

My place. His place.

His truck behind O'Gallaghers.

In the shower. On the kitchen counter. The stairs leading to my bedroom.

I cannot get enough of this man and it seems the feeling is reciprocated.

"Fuck, fuck, yes, yes," I moan, dropping my head until my forehead is pressed into a pillow on my bed. Jake's hands hold my hips as he takes me from behind, pounding into me as I slam my hips back into him. We've learned if we want this position to last at all, it's just him—and mine or his hands when it's time.

The moment clit stimulation comes into play, I'm done.

Suddenly my hair is tight against my scalp as he fists it. He tugs gently and I arch up until I'm kneeling. With my hair in his grasp, Jake's other hand cups my neck and he applies the slightest of pressure.

"Touch yourself," he demands and I don't bother playing.

I need release too badly. I'm ready.

I reach between my legs and quickly strum my clit as he continues fucking me, holding me in place by my hair and neck. "Good girl," the growl of his voice directly in my ear tells me how close he is. "You about to come, baby?"

"Y-yes." I push the back of my head against his shoulder, my eyes squeezed shut.

Instead of finishing the job, he roughly pulls out and I drop forward onto the bed. Before I can make sense of the sudden position change, my ankles are being tugged and I'm rolled over. Jake's standing beside the bed now, and when my eyes meet his, he drops to his knees.

"Jake," I say his name with a gasp as his mouth closes directly on my clit. His tongue plays expertly over and around the bundle of nerves and I reach down to thread my fingers through his silky hair. He grunts his satisfaction but doesn't let up.

Neither of us cares when my phone starts to vibrate against the nightstand. It's been ringing off and on for the last two hours.

One, it's hardly six in the morning. The only people calling in the middle of the night or early morning hours are drunk. Or were in an accident.

Which is why I looked the first and second times it rang.

But it's only been Josh.

I took him out of my contacts but never blocked his number. It hadn't been necessary. Hell, he never responded to my text calling things off!

I haven't heard from the man in months and here he is,

calling in the early morning hours of a weekend? The man was easily drunk dialing me and I'm not interested.

We *have* kept my phone face up though so either Jake or I can easily see the caller ID—just in case it's someone calling for something actually important.

At the moment though, neither of us is in a position to see the phone and I don't care. I'm too close...

Needing more, I lift my feet to rest at the edge of the mattress but it's not comfortable so instead, I place them on Jake's broad shoulders.

Ah. Much better.

It's even *better* when Jake reaches up to grasp and knead my breast, but it's when he scissors my nipple between his fingers that has me shouting his name as my body shudders.

In our days of learning each other's bodies, I've discovered Jake really likes to fuck me as I'm coming apart around his cock so I'm not surprised in the least when he removes his mouth and I'm instantly filled with his hard, thick girth.

It only takes him a couple of pumps before his body tightens over mine.

"Shit, I'm going to miss this," he mumbles against my shoulder a little bit later after discarding the condom.

Smiling lightly, because I'll miss it too, I run my fingers over the shaved portion of his head. "It's only a couple of days." My smile is wiped from my face when my phone once again goes off. "Jesus," I groan, reaching blindly for the device. "He is fucking insistent."

Like every other time it's gone off in the last two hours, it's Josh.

"May I?" Jake asks, rolling to his side and holding a hand out.

"Have at it." Maybe if he hears I'm with a man, he'll

give up. Why the hell he's decided tonight was the night to start calling again, I have no idea.

And frankly, I don't care.

Josh hasn't taken a *fraction* of my attention in recent weeks. Jake keeps my mind plenty occupied.

Not at all concerned about Jake answering my phone, I snuggle into his body as he accepts the call and puts the cell to his ear. "Hello?" He trails his fingers up and down my spine and even without the phone being on speaker, I can hear my ex.

Or whatever the hell he was.

"Who the fuck are you?"

"The name's Jake. Got a reason you're calling my girl so many fucking times in the early morning hours?"

"Put Sophia on the phone."

"Can't. She's busy."

"It's six in the morning."

"And you've been calling her since four. She's getting sleep. She was up all night."

I chuckle lightly—he's not wrong about being up all night—but press my mouth into Jake's chest to muffle the sound. The laugh turns to a gasp though when he slides his hand down to my ass, grasping the flesh in a way that has goosebumps popping up all over my body.

Well, shit.

Now he knows I'm sensitive where my ass meets my upper legs. I can only imagine what he'll do with that information. Probably lick it...

"Well, wake her up and tell her it's important."

"Why don't you tell me and let me be the judge of how important it is?"

"Fuck you, asshole."

Jake pulls the phone back and looks at the screen. "He

hung up." He rolls me to my back so he can place the phone on the nightstand again but then goes back to his side. I just roll along with him.

I'm seconds from falling into a blissful nap when the doorbell chimes throughout the townhouse.

"That fucking ass," I groan, rolling away from the warm body beside me. I wouldn't put it past Josh to keep ringing it, over and over. It's rude and disrespectful at this hour.

I don't know what I ever saw in the guy.

I stomp my feet toward the bathroom to grab my Target-brand satin robe, pulling it on and tightening the belt before pulling open my bedroom door and racing toward the front door. Emina's bedroom door is opening as I clear the level and I wave her off. "It's Josh," I tell her.

"What?" Her sleepy reply comes out confused, and I don't blame her. As I round the banister for the stairs that descend toward the front door, I see Em look above me.

Jake is close on my heels, I'd guess.

"Do not open that door until I'm there," Jake threatens but when I look over my shoulder, he's caught up. "Don't know what the fuck he wants." He put on his boxers but nothing else.

Because he was in a hurry and wanted to catch up, or because he was looking to possibly intimidate Josh?

I don't care which. I'm just glad he's behind me.

I look through the peephole first to make sure it is the man who's been blowing up my phone for the last few hours.

Yep. It is.

I unlock both the deadbolt and knob locks, then open the door.

"Soph," he mumbles, reaching for me. I take a step back and Jake stops me from stumbling, wrapping an arm possessively around my upper body. "Who the fug are you?" Between Josh's heavily bloodshot eyes and rumpled clothes, I'd guess he drank the night away.

"Sophia's man," Jake answers. "You're drunk, dude. Go home and sleep it off." I give Jake points for not going all alpha on Josh.

"Not drunk," he scoffs. I swear, the man stands taller. Does he throw his shoulders back and chest out, too? Good Lord...

"Soph, I need you," Josh tries again, whining, and I shake my head.

"We're over, Josh. We've *been* over."

"I need you though! I made a mistake.."

Jake chuckles, his chest shaking against my back. *Heck, I could melt into this man.* "You've made a few of those, I've heard."

"Shut the fug up, you fugging asshole!" Josh's voice raises and he goes from an annoying drunk to an almost scary one when he pairs the yell with a fist to the door jam.

I startle but otherwise, try not to show I'm affected. "Josh! It's six in the morning," I scold quietly as if he were a child. "On a Sunday, no less. People are freaking sleeping. Go. Home. I'm not interested in whatever you're here to sell. Maybe Shaina or Megan will be. They seemed to like you enough before. Now, goodbye." I reach for the door to try and shut it on his face but his hand slaps out to halt the movement.

"Shaina was a mistake, darlin'," he moans, his attitude once again shifting. "I shouldn't have fucked her. You clearly would have come around eventually." His eyes dart to Jake and it doesn't take a genius to hear the inebriated dig for what it is.

He knows I'm sleeping with Jake—I mean, it's pretty

obvious if you're basing it on Jake answering Josh's phone call, or his arm possessively around my upper body as he stands behind me, half-naked.

"No shit, Sherlock. You don't step out on a good woman. Remove your hand." Jake's hold of me tightens a fraction and I get the feeling he's getting ready to put me to the side and deal with things himself if need be.

"Goodbye, Josh," I repeat, successfully closing the door on him this time. There are two pounds on the door as if he slammed both fists into it but I don't care.

That said, I do care forty minutes later when Jake and I have finished breakfast and I'm walking him out. I need a nap and to wrap up some work projects before Emina and I leave Wednesday, and Jake has the opening shift at O'Gallaghers.

He kisses me once at the bottom of the stairs but when he opens the front door, his upper body tenses. "Stay inside," he instructs over his shoulder.

Frowning, I try to look around him. "Why?"

"He's still here."

I roll my eyes heavenward and send up a prayer for good graces because I'm more than irritated now. Josh had plenty of opportunities to make things right. Hell, he had the opportunity to not sleep with my friend. Or friends, because I may not know the true number, but I have a suspicion he fucked more than just Shaina.

"Just don't...beat him up or anything," I mumble, stepping back toward the stairs. "I'd rather you not end up in jail."

He glances at me. "I make no promises."

"Jake."

When he twists and leans down, I take the goodbye kiss

he offers and rub my thumb over his stubbled cheek. "I'll see you later."

UNKNOWN NUMBER:

Please talk to me

UNKNOWN NUMBER:

I need you!

UNKNOWN NUMBER:

My parents are expecting you to join me on friday

UNKNOWN NUMBER:

Sophia. Please. Answer.

I TURNED my phone to "Do Not Disturb" an hour ago because the incoming messages kept distracting me from work. Initially, I went from sound, to vibrate, then to silent —and the phone illuminating while silent was still too much. Full DND was the only way I could focus.

Taking a break from my last video edit, I open my texts to see if anyone of importance—Mom, Dad, Jake...heck, even Emina, regardless of the fact she's literally downstairs —tried contacting me while in DND mode but all I'm being bombarded with are messages from Josh.

There are at least twenty unread ones. The desperation in his words coming and going, some more frantic than others, with the "others" being downright rude and mean.

Another comes through as I hold the device in my hand.

I don't mean to read it, but some of the words pop out at me, snagging my attention. My body heats in momentary embarrassment at those words, but I suck in a deep breath through my nose and attempt to convince myself nothing he says can affect me.

Yet another message in the same vein comes through. He's on a roll, it would seem.

UNKNOWN NUMBER:

> Your a fucking whore I know where he works you slept with him drunk off your ass but wouldnt so much as suck my cock????? Fuck you sophia you fucking slut

And that, my friends, is how your number gets blocked.

I am not dealing with this, I think, doing what I should have done many weeks ago.

Knowing he has zero power over me and I will no longer be troubled by his suddenly frequent messages, I turn my phone back into regular mode and put the ringer back on. I should break for lunch soon, which has me thinking about Jake.

The clock tells me it's almost noon, which means he's been at the pub for almost two hours. Part of me wants to sit at O'Gallaghers and watch him work, maybe snack on bar food that's terrible for you. But the other part knows we've spent practically every waking hour together in the last two weeks and we're coming up on a six-day break.

Briefly I wonder if it would be healthy to start putting distance between us now in preparation for the trip. Maybe this whirlwind is just heightened emotions, and the break will highlight that it's been nothing but a rebound.

But hell, I love being in Jake's presence. He makes me feel...everything.

Beautiful. Heard.

He makes me feel like I matter to him.

My mind made up, I shut down my laptop and grab the

keys to my car. I have an uneasy feeling thanks to Josh showing up early this morning, and figure driving will be safer than walking to O'Gallaghers.

Not that I'm afraid of Josh exactly but...

I don't know. I just don't feel great about the entire situation.

"I'm heading to O'Gallaghers," I announce once I hit the main level. Emina sits at the kitchen peninsula, working on her laptop. "You want to come with me? Ben's working." They've been spending more time together too, but as far as I'm aware, they're still in "hanging out" territory.

She looks at me and grimaces. "I probably shouldn't..."

"Girl, I just did the same thing. C'mon. Let's go. Please? Keep me company?"

"Ugh. Fine. But you owe me."

Laughing because I didn't have to try very hard to convince her, I start down the lower staircase. I can see both locks on the front door are secure and go into the garage instead. Emina joins me in the car only a few minutes later and we head into town.

"We should probably stop by Sprouts, too, on the way back. Load up on plane snacks," Emina says as she thumbs through her phone.

"Oo, Australian licorice," I moan, thinking of the chewy red candies Sprouts sells in bulk.

"I was thinking more along the lines of everything seasoned nuts, but you do you," she chuckles.

It doesn't take but five minutes to get to O'Gallaghers and we're lucky to snag a parallel parking spot I can just drive into. No back-and-forth wiggling for me.

Inside, it's busier than I thought it would be for a Sunday but isn't packed, by any means. Then again, the NBA finals started yesterday and the road to the Stanley

Cup begins tomorrow. O'Gallaghers will be hopping for the next couple of months.

We manage to find seats at the front bar, thanks to Ben's watchful eye. When we walked in, I saw as he asked someone to move down a seat so two stools would be available.

"Thank you," Emina says, taking a seat. He responds to her by winking.

Looking around, I don't see Jake anywhere. Ben's at the bar and a woman I recently met named Colie seems to be the one working the floor.

"You ladies want something to eat?" Ben asks, placing two glasses of ice water in front of us before beginning a pour of bottled white wine for Em. It's not the first lunch visit we've made and it's not his first time serving us. "We got tater tots in the order yesterday."

The man speaks my language. There's nothing better than good tater tots. "Oh, yes. I'll do those," I nod. "Maybe a grilled cheese, too?"

"Sure. Texas toast or brioche?"

I have to take a moment to consider the options but end up deciding on the brioche.

"Em?" Ben looks at her as he places her wine glass in front of where she sits.

"Barbeque sliders?"

"That a question or is it what you want?" he teases.

"Shush. I wasn't sure if they were available."

"Chicken or pork?"

"Chicken. I don't eat pork."

"Ah. Right. Forgot." He turns to punch items into the point-of-sale screen. "I'll let Jake know you're here."

"You don't have to," I wave off. "He'll figure it out eventually."

Eventually turns out to be ten seconds later, as he pushes through the swinging door. Instead of walking behind the bar, he walks to my side and I grin up at him before accepting his quick kiss.

"I was finishing up inventory counts and looked up at the camera monitors," he explains. "You didn't tell me you were coming."

"Last minute decision."

"Kind of impulsive, too," my friend offers.

"We drove. Before you ask."

He rubs his hand in a small circle between my shoulders. "I was actually going to ask if Josh was still hanging around the complex."

"No. Not that I noticed."

"Good. I had words with him and told him you'd be filing a restraining order if he continued to harass you."

"Jake..." I try not to let his words ruin the good mood I worked hard at keeping, yet they're a stark reminder of the multiple texts I received. Part of me knows blocking Josh's number is only a temporary measure but I don't want to give energy to the situation. I'd rather be blissfully unaware.

I feel him press a kiss to my head before he steps away. "That behavior only escalates, Soph."

Now would be a good time to tell him about the messages but I fear talking about them makes them, and the situation, more real. And the more real it feels, the more my heart pounds and my hands sweat. It's not a feeling I enjoy.

Besides, it's not like Jake can do anything.

"I blocked his number," I say instead, watching him move behind the bar.

"If that doesn't stop him, you really should consider contacting the police. Just to be safe." He braces his hands on the pine. "I'll keep an eye on your place while you two are away."

"Ben was going to take the Things to your apartment," Emina answers, using the group nickname the kittens got while being fostered by Ben. "There won't be anything of value in the apartment."

I try to think of easy things we can do besides a restraining order—because that feels like a bit much. "Should we install a camera or something? I mean, I'm not afraid of him, by any means. I think he's just butt-hurt. We could maybe get a security system? They have those for rentals and I think they can be set-up pretty quickly?"

"I won't lie," he tries to cover his worried look with an off-center grin, "it would make me feel better if you had eyes outside and a way to alert you. He called for *hours*, Soph. And when that wasn't enough, he camped out in front of your door. But I also don't think you guys need to have that worry while being on your trip."

"What if we set it up and for the time being, only you have access to the app?" I offer.

He drops his chin and levels me with an incredulous look. "You're telling me you won't download the app and check yourself, again and again, when you're supposed to be working *and* enjoying yourself?"

"She totally would," Emina supplies, at the same time I refute, "I wouldn't!"

Looking at her, I give her a light backhanded slap to her shoulder. "I wouldn't. I trust Jake." I turn my attention to him. "I trust you. And I trust between you and Ben, everything will be fine, and if it's not fine, you'll let us know." Then, because I hate feeling like an inconvenience and my feelings are starting to run all over, I add, "But I don't need your permission to put safety measures in place, and I don't need your opinion on whether or not I'm allowed to download an app to my phone."

"Rawr," Emina whispers to my left.

His eyes pinch at the corners as he leans further over the bar. With his voice low, he says, "I care about you."

"I know." He makes it evident in every move he makes. Everything he says. Everything he does.

"I just want you safe."

"He was drunk, Jake." Even I know that's just an excuse and doesn't give Josh permission to treat me the way he has. He may have been drunk at four in the morning, five, then six...

But what about when he was texting me an hour ago?

Surely he wasn't drunk then.

He was just an angry asshole.

I have to remind myself of that—that Josh had been angry—because I can't get that last text message out of my head.

"I don't care, Sophia." Jake shakes his head but keeps his voice low. "Set up the security system. Look at it while you're gone, if you really want to. And if he doesn't try anything, then we can laugh about how protective I am when it comes to you." He dips his chin to pin me with his gaze. "Because baby, that part's not changing."

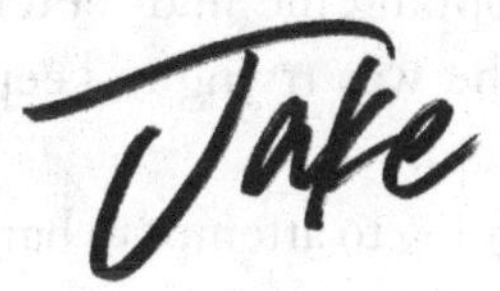

FIFTEEN

I HALF-EXPECTED Soph to announce she was through with me by the time Wednesday rolled around. I'd taken Monday and Tuesday off to spend time with her but on Monday, any time I tried to help with, hell, anything—packing, cooking dinner so she could finish edits, putting together the alarm system and camera doorbell that came via Amazon Prime—she brushed it off. She did, however, let me download the app and connect the doorbell to my phone, only for the sake of them being out of town and unable to do anything from across the world.

As I left Monday night, telling her I'd come back the next day, she told me she'd just be working and not bother coming by.

It would be "boring."

Even when I offered to simply keep her company and that I'd never be bored in her presence, she shook her head and said no.

In a matter of days, she shut me out.

Built walls sky high and locked the door.

Had I overstepped?

Should I have just let her figure out the Josh thing on her own?

Hell. What I *should* have done was tell her about Sunday morning when I escorted Josh off the property, regardless of her stopping me mid-sentence to tell me she wasn't interested. She was trying to keep the Josh chapter firmly closed, she'd said.

Do I think he's going to attempt to harm her in any way?

Nah. Not really.

He seems like a preppy punk kid who doesn't like to hear the word 'no.'

But I'd rather not put Sophia—or Emina, for that matter—in harm's way if he does decide to act out.

The only sliver of hope I had that our relationship was going to be okay was when she agreed to let me be their ride to the airport.

It didn't stop the cloud of dread hanging over my head, though. *Goes well with the clouds pouring rain all around us.*

Because of the weather, we took Sophia's car instead of my truck. I haven't installed the bed cover I bought a few months ago yet, and the backseat would be incredibly cramped for Emina if she had to share it with their luggage.

Should have done that yesterday, instead of sulking around the house worried I fucked up the one thing going well for me in life.

I pull up to an open spot in the unloading zone after a mostly silent car ride and push the button turning on the car's hazard lights. Both girls are pushing open their doors as I hit the trunk release, but they let me pull their bags out.

"Thanks," Emina says with a smile, reaching for her suitcase as she shoulders a backpack. She looks at Soph. "Do you want...?" Her eyes move to me briefly before landing back on Sophia.

Soph nods and Emina rolls her bag away and toward the sliding doors that lead into the airport, leaving me with my girl.

At least, I hope she's still my girl.

Her eyes are cast downward as she reaches for her suitcase handle. Needing to do something with my hands, I reach up to pull the trunk hatch down, the sound of it slamming in place seemingly louder than it is.

"Be safe, okay?"

She looks up at that and nods. "We will."

"I'd say take great footage, but I know you will." After watching her in action, my only conclusion as to why she doesn't film more is she has something in her brain telling her she's not good enough. I'm not exactly a connoisseur in videography, but I think she's damn talented behind a lens.

"If not, I'll just edit the hell out of it," she tries to tease, but her eyes quickly dart away as her lips pinch together into a tight line. When she blinks, a tear cascades down her cheek.

"Fuck, don't cry, Soph," I mumble, reaching for her out of necessity. She doesn't fight my embrace, so I give her a comforting squeeze. "I'm sorry—"

"Why are *you* sorry?" Her chuckle is watery as she works her arms up between us, moving to wipe at her eyes. "I'm the one who was a bitch the last two days." When she glances back in my direction, more tears fall.

I feel each drop like a vise tightening around my heart.

"I'm sorry for pushing. You're more than capable of taking care of yourself, I know."

"I'm not used to having someone who cares like you do," she whispers, her eyes locked on my chest. "I went from one extreme to another, and hell, I'm so freaking comfortable with you—"

"That's not a bad thing, baby."

"I know." She nods, as if convincing herself. But then she lifts her eyes to mine. "I know it's not a bad thing. I'm just scared." The last words are so soft, I nearly miss them.

My gut says she's not talking entirely about the Josh situation.

Rubbing my hands up and down her arms, I ask, "What scares you?"

She clenches a fist against her chest. "How much I feel," her broken words are as soft as her last. "And then Josh's..." She stops herself before swallowing hard. "What if while I'm gone, you find someone else? What if you find someone else to help and you fall for her instead?" The subject change catches me off guard and I frown, although maybe they're connected by whatever Josh texted her.

"You're going to be gone for six days, Soph. Not even a full week. We'll get through it. I promise."

"But what if—"

"Soph," I cut her off, taking her face in my hands. Her eyes are wild with emotion and unshed tears. "I'm not going anywhere. There is no one else for me," I try to say as pointedly as I can. "I will be here. And when you get back, I'm going to spend the next week showing you how much I missed you because I know I'm going to miss the hell out of you. Yeah, we went from zero to sixty pretty quickly, all things considered. But fuck if I'm not falling in love with you." Speaking of scared, I rush past that bombshell before she can shut it down. "I will do everything in my power to make sure you stay safe and don't get hurt on my watch.

And that means here too." I gently tap my index finger against her temple. "I don't care if Josh never lays a hand on you. The fact he's taken so much of your mental space over the last three days? That's what I care about."

"It's not that. Not really. He just said some things…" Her eyes close and I feel more than hear her exhale. "I blocked him, but he texted some not very nice things and they've just been playing over and over in my head."

I knew it. "What did he say?"

"You don't want to know…"

"If they've bothered you enough to be the reason you put space between us? Yeah. I want to know." I try to not let my own emotions come through but fuck, am I pissed at the asshole. "But I also respect that you don't want to share them with me, because babe, whatever he said is a lie."

"I just—"

She's interrupted by an agent blowing a whistle. "Gotta move it along, guys," he says.

Sighing, my hands once again framing her face, I rub my thumbs over the apples of her cheeks. "Be safe, baby, okay? Don't worry about Josh or the apartment or hell, not even me. It will all be okay and come Monday, you'll get back and things will be good as new, okay?"

She nods, giving a whispered, "Okay," before I tip her head back and lower my mouth to hers. Her hands wrap around my wrists and it almost feels like she's holding on for her life.

Damn, going without for damn near sixty hours felt too long. These next six days will be torture.

It's not the right time or place to take the kiss further. Instead, I pull away slowly until I can rest my forehead to hers. "I meant what I said," I tell her, in a chicken-shit way of re-confessing I love her. "I'll see you on Monday. Text whenever you want, call if you can...but definitely let me know when you land and then before your flight leaves."

Her hazel eyes, rimmed with red from tears, don't blink as she nods. "I will."

I press one more kiss to her forehead and step away. "Bye, baby."

THE DAY GOES PRETTY SMOOTHLY.

Sophia texted when they had a short layover in Seattle, but their next flight was twelve hours long. I wish I could say knowing she was in the air while I worked a double made my shift go quickly but it did not.

I couldn't stop replaying her words, over and over.

"You're preoccupied tonight," Cash mentions as we pass in the back, him for the floor and me for my final break of the night. "You okay?"

Nodding, I take a bite of one of the shalaylees I snagged from Hank as he began shutting down the grills and fryers. "Soph and Emina left for their trip this morning."

"You've got it bad," he chuckles, pushing the sleeves of his O'Gallaghers-branded long-sleeve tee up. "What's it been? A month?"

Has it only been a month? It sure as hell feels longer. But...

"I guess. We met right before St. Patrick's Day." Maybe that's what happens when you find the right person. Time ceases to exist—or rather, it simply flies by because you want nothing more than to spend every moment with that person.

"Her ex was fucking with her head the last couple of

days and things got a little rocky," I admit. "Bad timing. How was that wedding?"

He doesn't call me out on the change of subject. "It's next weekend. We've talked here and there and she bought my plane ticket so..." He shrugs. "Looks like it's happening."

"Where's it at?" I'd assumed it was local.

"New York. I guess the bride's a cousin and her extended family won't get off her back about being single."

Chuckling at how crazy the whole thing sounds, I shake my head. "Good luck with the charade."

"Hey, I know her adult beverage of choice. I can walk up to her while she's talking with her family and hand her her drink. None will be the wiser."

"Fucking absurd," I snicker as we part ways.

It's just after ten and although I know the girls won't land at their second layover for another hour, I look at my phone anyway.

And am surprised to see a message from Soph.

SOPH:

I napped on it and I'm going to show you these as long as they go through.

SOPH:

Maybe they won't send. Ugh.

SOPH:

-image-

SOPH:

Okay just slow wifi.

SOPH:

-image-

SOPH:

-image-

SOPH:

I think our next layover is just over an hour but depending on immigration and the airport not sure how much time we'll have. I'll try calling if there's time.

I recognize the screenshots as text conversations and off the bat know they're the ones she got from Josh.

As badly as I want to see the words that caused her to put walls up, I'd rather respond to Sophia when I'm of level mind. I scroll past them for the moment.

Holding my last shalaylee with my mouth, I use both hands to type out a reply.

ME:

I work until 1230 tonight. That's about two hours from now, assuming you'll get this message right away or it will time stamp correctly. *fingers crossed emoji* hopefully timing works *fingers crossed emoji*

Plopping down in the office, I finish the makeshift meal and wipe my fingers on my jeans, ready to open the images but Sophia responds right away.

SOPH:

Okay.

SOPH:

kiss emoji

SOPH:

I'm sorry again.

ME:

I'm sorry you have an ass of an ex.

SOPH:

Did your message come late? Are you off now? I could open the time converter page but I'm too lazy. Emina's been sleeping and I've already watched the only movies I was interested in...

ME:

Nope, just on a break. Just sent that message so you must be pretty realtime right now.

ME:

Obviously you're realtime. We're having a conversation *winky face emoji*

SOPH:

Oh so maybe when we land it will time perfectly with you heading home. That's be nice.

SOPH:

that'd**

ME:

Agreed

SOPH:

Did you look at them?

ME:

No. I wanted to talk to you more...

SOPH:

Well when you do look at them I promise I'm trying to not let them bother me

Bubbles appear as if she's writing something else, but they stop and reappear twice as I type out my response.

ME:

I see that 'try'

SOPH:

I just thought if this is going to work then i need to be willing to trust yo u and sharing them doesnt mean i thinkyoure going to get all pissy and overstep but that youll understand wy i shut down

It looks as if she rushed that comment and hit 'send' before she could think better of it. I can't help but smile a little as I lean forward, hunched and resting my elbows on my knees with my phone in both hands. I'm thinking Sophia is 100% in now, although I hate that she's worried about my reaction to words from an angry asshole who thought it was okay to cheat on her.

But is it my reaction that has her nervous, or is she afraid I'll believe the words Josh said? That I'll agree with him? My smile falters.

SOPH:

You're something else Jacobi Wesley

ME:

Still think it might be a red flag?

SOPH:

Brazil flag emoji *Brazil flag emoji* *Brazil flag emoji*

Chuckling, the strong need to ease any worries she may have, I respond with comedy.

ME:

What's Brazil got to do with it?

ME:

winky kiss face emoji

SOPH:

laughing with tears of joy emoji

ME:

I unfortunately have to get back on the floor but thank you for trusting me with those, Soph. Thank you for trusting me with YOU

SOPH:

heart emoji

Her lack of more words doesn't bother me. If anything, it tells me she's feeling overwhelmed but, ideally, in a good way.

I send her a heart emoji back and debate looking at the screenshots, but decide it's probably not a good time. I don't want to be pissed on the floor for my last two hours.

Later will be soon enough.

SIXTEEN

IT DOESN'T TAKE LONG to get to our next gate once we arrive in Incheon. Because our final connecting flight is also an international one, we don't need to claim and recheck bags so we have more time than I thought we would.

It's a neat airport, with funky architectural designs and real plants and trees. We've taken several selfies already and have laughed at the shadows and bags under our eyes.

"May we always remember how long this day was," Emina had joked when she sent me the latest images.

After grabbing food, we find a counter with various plugs available for device charging and are once again sitting, this time to eat our dinners. I know I should eat. Our next flight is seven hours long and I'm kind of over plane food—even with the fancier options premium seating affords. But I have too much on my mind and I no longer think my stomach twisting has to do with hunger and instead, is worry about Jake's reaction to what I sent him a couple of hours earlier.

Regardless of all that and me telling him I'd call if there was time while at the airport, I *want* to hear his voice. Perhaps *need*.

"Do you mind if I call Jake?"

Emina shakes her head as she bites into a dumpling, allowing the steam to escape. She's preoccupied with a book she's been reading on her phone.

The clock changed on my cell when we landed and shows it's five in the afternoon. I'm too exhausted to try and figure out what time it is in San Diego. Hopefully, he answers. I don't think it's been much longer than two hours since we messaged last.

I'm surprised at how much I miss him, even though it's only been twelve hours since we left San Diego.

Too much, too fast, too soon... My head wars with my heart.

As the phone rings in my ear, I unwrap my burger and fries—from Shake Shack because I'm a little shell shocked by all the food and I don't have what some would call a "worldly palate."

He answers just as I pop a fry into my mouth.

"Hey, babe." The noise behind him sounds like the heavy back door to O'Gallaghers opening and closing, but just the sound of his voice, his own exhaustion evident, has the lead in my stomach easing.

"Are you just getting off work?"

"I am. Well, I did a little while ago but stuck around so I didn't fall asleep before you called. It's been a long day."

With a short chortle, I eat another fry. "You're telling me."

"Can't decide if 14 hours on two planes is worse than

twelve hours at O'Gallaghers," he jokes. "But that's a long-assed time to sit."

I didn't sit the entire time but there are bonus points to sitting in premium and getting a leg rest.

"Was it busy tonight? Or today?" I nibble on my dinner as we talk. My internal clock isn't thrilled about eating something heavy at what is usually midnight—the time based solely on the fact Jake is only leaving O'Gallaghers now.

"It was. It was game seven for the Enforcers so we had a lot of fans. Were you able to follow it at all, or do you want me to tell you the score?"

Grinning, I nod even though he can't see.

God, the way he makes me feel. The way he knows me...

"Yes, please. I totally forgot it was game seven. Did they advance? Tell me they advanced."

Jake's chuckle through the phone is all I need to feel awake and myself again. Sure, the euphoria may have a little to do with the prospect of my hockey team advancing in the postseason but mostly, it's *him*.

"They did. Shut out. Five-nothing with two empty netters at the end."

"Are you serious? Game seven and a shutout?" Emina glances at me as my voice raises in excitement. "Who was in goal? JP?"

"Jonny? Yeah."

"How freaking awesome. Ugh. I wish I could have watched it."

"Do they not have live TV on the flights?"

"They do but I didn't notice any sports. It was mostly news and home and garden kind of shows."

There's a small break in talking so I lift my burger and take a small bite. The bread and meat feel heavy in my mouth and my stomach is already rolling in protest. Emina's soup with dumplings was probably a better idea but broth didn't seem filling at the time—and I don't do dumplings.

Chewing and swallowing, I re-wrap the majority of the sandwich and just snack on fries.

I'm pretty sure I hear Jake yawn. The drive home from O'Gallaghers isn't terribly long but if I can keep him talking and awake, I'm happy to do it.

If only there weren't nerves knocking on my mind, wanting to know if he took a moment to look at the messages Josh sent me.

"So, um... Did you get a chance to look at them?"

When I sent the screenshots, it was because I wanted to keep an open door of trust and communication with Jake after practically shutting down on him for two days. I told myself I didn't care what his reaction was.

Told myself whatever his reaction was wouldn't change a thing.

The shameful words wouldn't take away those three words he slipped into our conversation at the airport.

He'd still be his self-proclaiming protective self and I'd still be on the other side of the world.

The sound of a vehicle door shutting fills the line, followed by the turning of an ignition. For a short second, music plays, too, but it's shut off quickly and silent once again.

"I did."

He doesn't expand.

"And...?" I draw out.

"My question for you is, do *you* believe his words?"

"No," I answer too quickly, and immediately *know* Jake will call me out on it.

"You sure?"

I move my tongue over the front of my top teeth before angling my body away from Emina. The gate area is beginning to fill with late-afternoon travelers. We're near enough to our departure gate that I can see the seats filling. There's not even every other seat available, as people want to sit and organize their carry-ons before travel. I wonder how many sitting there are for our flight, and how many are there already for the following one.

"What about what he said is hurting you the most?" Jake presses gently when I don't answer.

My throat tightens and my eyes start to itch. Pinching the bridge of my nose, I look down and squeeze my eyes shut. *I'll blame this moment on the exhaustion,* I tell myself. After all, I was the one who brought it up.

I wanted to talk to him about the messages.

Just a glutton for punishment, Sophia...

But *I* wanted to fix the lack of communication.

I wanted to show him I trusted him.

And I'd be lying if I didn't confess I needed to hear him say that Josh's words were a lie. That he read them and didn't believe them. Would never believe them.

That I'm not the things Josh said I am.

"I don't want to cry right now, Jake," I plead quietly into the phone.

The line is silent and I fight the urge to see if he hung up, although I know he didn't. He wouldn't.

"I think he's an asshole," Jake finally says, as if carefully weighing his words. "And I think he wanted to lash out at you because he figured you were an easy target. Don't be an easy target, Soph."

My voice low, I try to make him understand. "It's just... the words..."

"Don't be an easy target," he repeats. "How long until your next flight?"

The topic transition isn't the smoothest but I'm thankful for it all the same. "We'll probably start boarding soon."

"Well then, let's take these last few minutes and make 'em worth it. I've never been on a flight longer than six hours. How terrible was it?"

My lips fight to turn upward. "It surprisingly wasn't terrible at all, although I didn't sleep much. The time went by faster than I thought it would."

He asked about the food we were served and laughed when I told him I had to pick through the last dinner on the flight.

"I don't suppose you're trying any Korean dishes while on your layover, are you?" I can hear the smile in his voice because he knows all too well I have the taste buds of a toddler.

"Nope. I grabbed Shake Shack."

"As in an American hamburger and french fries?"

"You bet."

Once again, his laugh calms me, mentally setting me on even ground again. I smile and eat a cold fry. "You home yet?"

"Just pulling into the complex. I'll take Boo for a walk and hit the sack. You guys boarding?" As he asks, Emina taps me on the shoulder and nods toward the gate.

"Yeah, looks like it's time." I gather my things and after tossing our trash, we move to stand in line, waiting for when it's our turn.

"Try to get some rest on the flight, 'kay? You guys land in Bali when? Midnight Friday morning, your time?"

"About then."

"So you should be able to get sleep before the wedding

stuff. But...try. Then you can hopefully enjoy Friday afternoon and sleep normally before the event."

"I will."

"All right, well. I guess I have to let you go."

"Thank you for dealing with the wheel of emotions." Our boarding group is called and I know I have to hang up. I just don't want to.

"I have sisters. I'm used to them," he explains, lightheartedly. "Love...'em." Was he about to say it again? That he loved me? After everything? "Can't wait for you to meet them. I know it will be late your time, but let me know when you guys land again, okay?"

"I will. Sleep well, Jake."

"You too. Mean it. Close your eyes on the plane."

It's difficult, but we manage to stop extending the conversation and hang up as it's my turn to show my boarding pass and passport.

The worry I had earlier lingers, but it's not quite as loud. Not as noticeable.

And my head's constant chant of *too much, too fast, too soon,* is quieter—allowing my heart to believe the timeline is just right.

Maybe it's because of the ease in my soul, but I fall asleep soon after takeoff. It's a dreamless sleep but I wake feeling refreshed. My blood no longer feels sluggish in my veins. Exhaustion still seeps in my bones though after traveling for so many hours.

Both Emina and I are quiet as we deplane, and only make mindless small-talk as we move through immigration and grab our bags at baggage claim.

There's even a gentleman with a sign for us, and he escorts us to the private car the bride and groom arranged.

It's only when we're finally headed to the resort that I think to take my phone out of airplane mode.

"I sure hope the beds are as comfortable as they look in their listings," Emina mumbles, shutting her eyes.

Agreed. I could use a nice seven-hour deep sleep.

And a hot shower.

"It's a world-class resort," I offer optimistically. "I'm going to guess the beds feel like clouds and come morning, we'll be more than ready to take on Bali." My friend's answer is soft *hmm* in confirmation.

Between Emina resting and a stranger driving, I decide I'm more comfortable sending Jake a text telling him we've made it, rather than calling. I open the messaging app, waiting as everything loads into place.

Before I can compose a message in our thread, a notification drops down telling me I have a voicemail.

Maybe it's because I'm exhausted and have been traveling all day, but the moment the notification bar drops down, I have flashbacks to Sunday and the very first thought that comes to mind is, *What if it's Josh?*

The thought is so sudden, so left field, that irrational nerves take hold of my body. Knowing it's silly doesn't stop my blood from chilling as my heart skips a beat.

Unfortunately, my call log doesn't show anything for the last seven hours. I know it's not Josh. Deep down, I *know* it's not him.

You blocked his number, Sophia, the rational part of my brain tries easing, while the other yells louder, *He can call from another number.*

It's more likely the message is from Jake. Heck, maybe even my parents, wanting to make sure Em and I got to Bali okay but not sure about the time difference.

No matter how much I try convincing myself it's safe to listen to the message, I can't make my fingers dial voicemail.

"Hey, Em?"

Rolling her head on the back of the seat, she opens her eyes slowly. "Hmm?"

I open my mouth, only to shut it again and frown. Shaking my head, I say, "Nevermind. It's something stupid. I know it's just my parents or Jake." Maybe saying it out loud will help.

She doesn't laugh at me. She doesn't tell me I'm probably right.

Instead, she holds out her hand. "You're afraid it's Josh, I'm guessing? Would it make you feel better if I listened to it first? At least long enough to let you know it's not him?"

"I know it's not..." The words don't come out nearly as strong as I hoped they would, but I hand the device over all the same.

"We're supposed to have fun this weekend. Well, and work, too," Em smiles softly at me, holding my phone to her ear. "If Josh ruins our trip, I will personally hunt him down when we get home and cut off his dick." She doesn't need to ask for my passcode when prompted and while the phone is to her ear, she uses her index finger to turn the volume down. "You're so deaf," she mumbles, her tired tone teasing. The seconds feel like minutes before she holds the phone out. "It's Jake. And I have to say, I'm a teeny bit envious."

Dropping my brows, I take it back. "Why?"

"Just listen."

Once she's free of her best friend duties, she crosses her arms over her chest and attempts to nap once again. I press the appropriate buttons to restart the message, increasing the volume a bit because, for whatever reason, I have a hard time hearing my phone when it's right next to my ear.

Angling away from Emina but only so I can lean semi-side-ways into the seat, I fixate my eyes on the darkness outside the car window.

"Hey, baby. I can't sleep. It's like...two here. I've been laying in bed and can't get my mind off you and the last couple of days. I think you're only like an hour into this last leg." He sounds as exhausted as I feel, as if sleep is just beyond his reach. *"If I mathed correctly, you'll land some-time around the time I get up but then you'll be exhausted one. I could save this for later when you call again or even when you're home, but I think you need to hear it as soon as possible. I know you won't fully enjoy yourself with every-thing lingering, and I think the reason I can't sleep is because the words won't leave me alone.*

"You are so beautiful, Sophia. Inside and out. Every minute I get to spend in your presence makes my day better. It doesn't matter if you're excitedly explaining something you're passionate about, or if you're sitting quietly, clearly lost in your head.

"But whether you're excited or lost, I will gladly stand in your corner, again and again. I will cheer you on when you set out on a new project and I will celebrate every success you have, because you will have a lifetime of success. You just have to believe it, too. Until you do, though, I'll believe in you enough for the both of us.

"I don't know that I ever told you, but I vividly remember the night we met...and I'm not talking about the end of the night. I can see you standing among everyone else. I can picture when your eyes met mine during I.D. checks. I have zero recollection of where Emina was in that group, everyone else is a blur. Well. Except Megan but that's because of her claws and she grabbed my ass. But you? You struck me right away and I don't even have to try remem-

bering where you were. What you looked like. Your demeanor. It's a clear snapshot in my mind.

"When you walked back into O'Gallaghers later, I was secretly thrilled to get to spend a little more time with you—and then you sat at the bar, which felt like a good sign. But it was quickly noticeable you weren't in a good place and I didn't want to pry. I walked you home because my gut told me it was important to do. I've never had the desire to walk someone home after a night of drinking. That is reserved solely for you, Sophia Burns.

"I need you to hear that, Soph, because it was something you said this morning...yesterday morning, I guess, at the airport. I have no intention, Soph, zero desire, to find someone else. I know it's been fast. Even Cash mentioned it earlier and it was like, holy shit, it's only been, what, a month? But fuck if I care. I look forward to every day, every week, every month, we get to spend together, learning more about each other, and in a few years, the first few weeks and how fast they were won't matter in the bigger scheme of the life we make."

I'm no longer noticing the few signs we pass or the stars in the sky. I'm completely lost in Jake's words. They're like a caress over bruised and battered skin. How does he always know what to say? I pinch my lips together.

I miss him.

I shouldn't have been so freaking stubborn this week. I should have taken those hours and trusted he'd know the right things to say and do to keep me and my emotions from imploding.

"But I also know you worry about it. I know you didn't want to jump into things quickly, and I know his words hit you in a spot that hurt. His words had your fears of moving too fast...they made those fears come to the surface. But

Sophia? They were just words spoken by an asshole you fucked once. Don't even give him the label of an ex because he's not worth having any spot in your history. He doesn't get a say in your life. He stopped getting that privilege the moment he so much as looked at another woman while he was supposed to be with you. His opinion of you...means nothing. He wasn't expecting you to have someone in your corner. He thought he could weasel his way back in and because you are who you are, and your beautiful mind works the way it does, he thought he could get you to agree to his ways. But he was wrong. Because that same beautiful mind also knows what she deserves...when you're not busy filtering out the negative self-talk.

"Any relationship worth lasting is going to have give and take, but I'll happily stay in the house with you, or do something low-key with only a couple of our friends, over parties and clubs and anything else that you think would drain you. I don't need to dress up and take you out, show you off, for me to know you care for me, and I hope it's the same for you. Besides, I really like your couch." There's the smallest of chuckles with his comedic relief, which has my lips tipping up ever so slightly. "I'll watch a movie there every night of the week I'm not working instead of going on a downtown date. Hands down. Tell me which of your favorite wines to bring over, and I'll be there with dinner, too.

"I'm not going anywhere, Soph. I will be here and I will be the person you need. The person you want. For however long you'll have me."

He takes in a deep breath and it sounds like it's followed by a yawn. "Have fun with Em this weekend. Trust that you have the ability to take bomb-ass video and believe you'll take that amazing-as-hell footage and put it together in a video the couple will cherish for the rest of their lives. And *when you close your eyes tonight, know this: I'm absolutely honored that you've chosen me to be your person. I will not take that responsibility lightly."* He pauses for a few seconds before he speaks again, bringing tears to my eyes—and I know it's not exhaustion causing them this time. *"I love you, Soph. Fuck time. I know what I feel isn't something I've felt before and I know it's not something that can be replicated. I love you and I'll be here, waiting for you to catch up. Be safe. I'll see you on Monday. Good night, baby."*

"He's a good one," Emina mumbles from her side of the car when the message ends and I put the phone in my lap. "You should probably keep him."

"I think I might."

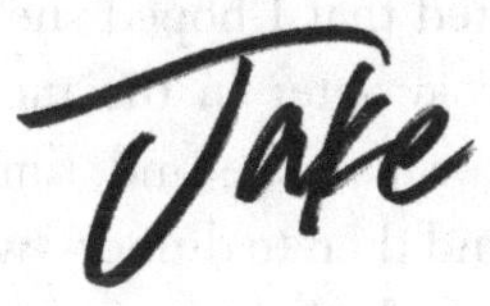

SEVENTEEN

THE TIME DIFFERENCE between San Diego and Bali leaves a lot to be desired. Sophia and I managed to talk yesterday—five p.m. here, eight a.m. there—and even though they'd only experienced bed and breakfast at that point, I was happy to hear the excitement in her voice again.

The doubt and worry were gone. At least, concerning Josh and that whole situation.

I'd tried really hard to read the texts as objectively as possible, but I won't lie; my emotions got the better of me. Except it wasn't appropriate to put those feelings on Soph, not when she already carried so much doubt because of them. Instead, I did what I could think to try and ease her mind by leaving a voicemail she could listen to, turn off if she needed, and wouldn't feel like she needed to respond to any part of it.

Being more forthcoming in my emotions for her was maybe a bit too much, but I hated the idea of her thinking anything the asshole said about her would change what I thought and felt for her.

We didn't discuss the voicemail but just hearing her sound like her normal, happy self was more than enough confirmation for me.

After that first phone call, I tried calling later when I left O'Gallaghers at two-thirty Friday morning but she didn't answer. I texted that I hoped she was having a good day, and when I woke later in the morning, she'd texted back, apologizing because she and Emina had gone to a monkey sanctuary and then to dinner—where she was brave and tried sate ayam, "which, to be fair, is chicken skewers," she'd added but I gave her points for trying something new, especially when she mentioned she'd had a taste of Emina's goat version, too.

The pictures she sent from their time at the sanctuary were amazing. Statues and bridges and overlooks, all within the confines of rich greens and soft browns. She'd also sent a picture of her laughing as a monkey perched on her shoulders, picking at flyaways around her face from her ponytail.

I couldn't blame her for not pulling her attention from the scenery and experience.

I called immediately after seeing the text, and this time she answered, but we quickly switched to a video call where she shared her view from the private infinity pool outside their room. It was nine at night and the forest was too dark to make anything out, but her smile as the water reflected up into her eyes was enough to ease my worries.

The woman smiling through the screen no longer looked like the one I left at San Diego International on Wednesday morning. The joy was back on her face.

It's too early in her day for me to call now. The clock widget I added to my phone says it's only four in the morning Bali time. Being it's her Saturday, I don't know if she'll have an opportunity to call at any point today, either. When I get off of work at one tonight, she'll be in the thick of wedding festivities, if the schedule she shared is followed.

That said, I do want to wish her luck—and give her some positivity to lean into before the big day.

ME:

Kick ass today. You're going to do great. REMEMBER. they wouldn't have hired you if they didn't think you were worth it no matter what Emina told them. Em showed them your work and they fell in love with YOU and YOUR footage

ME:

I'm working until 1 here which is 3 in the afternoon for you but I'll call when I get up in the morning. Text me if you want.
Love you.

I don't think twice before ending the text with it. That's not to say I don't stare at the words and worry I'm coming on too strong. She hasn't repeated them and I'm trying not to let it bug me. She's had a whirlwind of a week and if I know anything about Sophia, it's that she needs to process things in her own time.

Ben doesn't work today so I don't rush to give Boo a walk before heading into town. I do, however, give her a cookie treat as I walk out the door.

Once in my truck, I take a second to debate if I should swing around to the back of the complex and run past Sophia and Em's.

Ben was just there to grab the Things' bed, I remind myself.

Convinced it's okay to leave, I head straight to work.

These long midday shifts Conor put me on this week haven't been too bad. I don't have to open and I don't have to close. I'm still at O'Gallaghers for twelve or so hours, which is an exhausting day—one I requested, I know—but not having the responsibility of being the shift lead has been a nice change of pace.

Two shifts down, three more to go. Let's see how I feel about them on Sunday.

I park where I always do and head inside, clocking in from the back office computer. After washing my hands in the kitchen's hand washing specific sink, I walk out to hit the floor—but my phone buzzes in the pocket of my jeans. Pausing my stride, I take a second to see who it is.

Turns out, it's not a call or a message.

It's a notification from the girls' doorbell.

It's probably just UPS or something.

I can't let it go without looking. I open the app and wait for the video to load, swearing when it starts to play.

Josh is outside their door.

Because of course, he is.

The dude can't get a hint.

He's dressed up—compared to the other morning, at least—and has a bouquet in his hand. *The fuck?* Once again, he rings the doorbell, shifting from foot to foot, before he seemingly gives up.

He turns on his heel and heads toward the gate, only to whirl around, tossing the flowers at the door.

"You clocked in, Wesley?" Shayne peeks around the swinging door she holds open.

"Yeah. Just..." I hold up a finger, my eyes trained on the screen. Josh doesn't seem to do anything else. Doesn't go back to the door, doesn't come back into the yard. In seconds, he's completely out of view of the small camera. I scroll the video forward the fifteen or so seconds of lag time to make sure he's not back and it seems to be all clear. The small gate is swinging open with the wind and the flowers remain on the ground, mostly out of view, but nothing else seems amiss.

"Sorry," I say, closing out of the app and putting my phone to sleep. "Sophia's ex showed up at her place."

"Do you need to do anything with that?"

I begin to tell her no but think twice about it. "Actually, let me text Ben real quick to clean it up, if that's okay?"

"Go ahead. I have you up on bar. I'll do office things when you get out."

After shooting Ben a message and receiving his immediate reply, I head onto the floor, ready to get the day started.

Unfortunately, the shift would only get worse from there.

HARDLY TEN MINUTES into being on the floor, with my back turned to get a customer's lunch order in the point of sale screen, I'm being pelted by pretzels.

"Hey!" Saint yells, as I turn to face the assailant.

"What the fuck?" It takes less than a second for me to recognize the person standing furiously on the other side of the bar, his hand holding the now empty red plastic basket, ready to launch it in my direction.

"Where is she?" Josh yells.

The patrons nearby glance between the three of us, and when Saint waves backward in a silent ask to move, they gladly do—with their drinks, of course.

"That's no business of yours," I try to keep my voice

calm, even when the basket is launched past my head. I dodge left but when a liquor bottle teeters on the shelf after being hit, I attempt to catch the glass before it crashes to the floor.

I nearly succeed but after three juggles, it falls, shattering on the ground.

Saint chuckles darkly behind the man, reaching for his arm. "You done fucked up now, man." Josh tries to fight him off but he's no match for Max St. James.

When he's secure, I kick the discarded basket out of the way and lean into the bar. "Listen, Josh. Any other person, and throwing shit at the staff just gets you kicked out and banned, but because you're you... I'll do you one better."

Likely having seen the commotion in the monitors, Shayne jogs out from the office just as I tell Josh I'm calling the police department on his ass.

"I've got it," Shayne offers, and I let her because I have more to say.

"Thanks," I tell her before resuming my conversation. But then Josh spits at me like he's a twenty-year-old kid who doesn't know what the hell to do with his testosterone.

"That's so fucking gross," Saint practically gags behind Josh, tightening his hold on the man.

I take my unused bar towel to wipe my face. "I'm not entirely sure why you think I'm the one you should be coming after," I tell him, eerily calm. Far calmer than I'd imagine I'd be in a circumstance such as this. "*You* are the one who fucked up. *You* are the one who slept around on her. As I told you the other morning, *she doesn't fucking want you*. She's moved on, man. Doesn't think about you, doesn't care about you, you don't fucking cross her mind. Let her move on. You think this childish behavior will get her to forgive you for fucking her friend? You don't know her very well."

"She would have if it weren't for you," Josh bristles, and I can't help but laugh humorlessly.

"You're fucking joking, right?"

"Lonely bitches always crawl back."

The anger I'm feeling must cross my face because both Shayne and Saint say my name in warning.

Beyond disgusted, I turn to retrieve the broom from the back. "Get him away from the bar."

It only takes the local PD five minutes to arrive and after they free Saint of the asshole, an officer takes my statement.

"While a protective order attached to you doesn't necessarily protect your girlfriend," the officer says after I break down the day and who Josh is in relation to me, "if she's with you and he tries to do something that breaks the order, it still works negatively in his favor and keeps your girlfriend safe. You said her name was Sophia Barnes?"

"Burns. B-U-R-N-S." We're sitting at a booth in the back corner, away from the patrons who are once again eating and drinking as if the last half hour was nothing.

"Got it," he murmurs, scribbling in his notepad. "I'll file my report and, just so you're prepared, criminal charges will likely move forward. With simple battery..." he shrugs a shoulder, "assuming it's his first offense...? Honestly, probably not much will come from it. It's more likely he'll be released today with the promise to return for arraignment on Tuesday, where he'll be slapped with a fine, maybe a few weeks behind bars. But filing a civil harassment restraining order at least puts some level of protection in front of you. Now, I know it's not manly to put a restraining order in place—"

I cut him off, "If it protects Sophia at all, I'm for it." My fingers drum an irregular beat on the tabletop, pent-up energy needing to be released in any way it can. "I brought up her getting one the other morning when he came to the house—"

The man's forehead wrinkles as his brows rise. "So this isn't the first meeting between the two of you?"

"No. As far as him and Sophia, he initially left her alone after the breakup but then Sunday he was calling in the early morning hours. Started just before four, I think? Maybe three. I was at her place."

"He was just calling?"

"At first, yes. Back to back calls. He'd break for a few minutes and then start again, but at six, he started ringing the doorbell. Soph answered the door, I was right there with her, and he tried grabbing at her. He was drunk and she didn't think anything would come of it. She put up a camera doorbell though, and he was by her place today before he came here. If you think it's helpful, I can download and send the video to you."

The officer takes a deep breath and sighs, his hands in an open-palm gesture. "While I'm not sure it will hold, I could suggest stalking, too. Then he *would* be held for forty-eight hours. No, forgive me. It's Friday evening. Seventy-two hours because of the weekend. I'll take that video and add it to the surveillance footage from here."

It doesn't take the officer much longer to wrap up with my statement. "I'll give you a call to let you know if he's being held or not. Might still be worth convincing Ms. Burns to get a domestic restraining order in place. These things only escalate."

I agree. "That's what I told her. Thank you, Officer."

"Not a problem. Like I said," he says, standing from the

table and pocketing his notebook, "I'll give you a call so you know what to expect."

———

I WISH I could say the night only got better from there.

The one bright point from today? Josh doesn't qualify for the cite and release and is being held until Tuesday. Not that I was worried about him coming back here to stir shit, but knowing he's locked up for a few nights means there won't be any more unannounced visits to the girls' place and no additional clean-up before they get back Monday. It also gives me time to talk to Sophia about the events and that's not something you text.

While there were a few steady hours and nothing out of the ordinary, it only took one phone call.

It remains semi-busy at midnight, but between this entire afternoon and Soph being out of the country, I remove my phone to see why it won't stop buzzing incessantly in my back pocket.

A text message notification from my mom flashes—and comes in as urgent—which is why the device keeps going off. "Hey," I off-handedly call out to Colie, who came in at six for the closing shift. "Do you mind if I check this?"

Her nod is quick as she steps behind the bar to cover for me. "Yeah. Not a problem."

After heading into the back, I open the text.

> YOUR MOTHER:
>
> Please call when you see this

A feeling of dread washes over me. First, she deliberately sent the message as urgent, but then to not put what was urgent *in* the message is enough for me to know it's something serious.

Is it Dad?

Did something happen to him?

One of my grandparents?

Or is it one of my sisters?

I take no time to press the call button and slide into the quiet office. It only rings once before the call opens, and, based on the sound of air and road noise, I'm on Bluetooth in the car.

"What's wrong?" I ask, bracing myself for the worst.

But it's not Mom who answers. It's Dad.

The relief at hearing his voice is sudden, but is quickly wiped away. "Hollis was in a bad car accident. We're headed to the hospital now."

"They just took her from the accident site," Mom adds shakily.

My mind goes wild with every scenario imaginable. "Is... Is she okay?"

"We don't know." Mom's reply is broken as a sob seems to cut through.

"We didn't get to see her," Dad supplies. "By the time we got the call, she was already being loaded into the ambulance. But the trooper said it wasn't good."

I glance at the clock even though I know it's just after midnight. "There won't be any flights out until morning."

"You don't have—"

"I will be there. It just won't be until probably noon." After five years in San Diego, I'm well-versed on the plane schedules. There aren't nonstop flights from San Diego to Billings. Not even from LAX—and I'd gladly make the two-hour drive if it meant I got home faster.

There's a slight beep over the line.

"That's Chandler," Dad shares.

"Does she know yet?"

"No."

I nod to myself, my eyes fixated on the wooden desk. "Okay, well. Talk to her. And please keep me updated. I'll be there tomorrow." Glancing at the schedule clipboard, I realize I have gross shifts to find coverage for, but if Hollis...

My sister's laughing smile fills my mind and I swear, I'm seconds away from tearing up. *Fuck!* I can't let myself think something terrible will be the result of tonight.

"Love you guys."

They reply in kind, then I let them deliver the bad news to my sister.

I can't get myself to stand up from the desk and go back to work. I can't stop picturing my youngest sister being thrown around in her car.

I can't stop imagining her '09 Accord being crushed in multiple fashions, again and again and again, as I berate myself for not asking more questions.

Did she roll? Was her car smashed into a median or a building?

Was it head-on, or single vehicle? Road rage?

Was it on purpose?

I mentally push the thought from my mind as soon as it hits. Chandler went through a dark period in high school when our family moved from Billings to Forever. It was my first year in college but I flew home on more than one occasion specifically because of Chandler.

Never was it Hollis.

It was never the bubbly, always smiling, Hollis.

"Fuck!" I groan, tossing my phone down on the desk and dropping my head back. My eyes are open, focused on the ceiling, when Cash comes to the office door.

"You good?"

I don't bother denying I'm not, grinding my molars together as I stand and retrieve my phone. "Nah. Not really."

"Sophia?" He frowns, and again, I shake my head.

"No, my youngest sister was in a car accident. I guess it's not good. I don't..." I jab my hands up into my hair. "I don't know anything. My parents don't know anything. They're heading to the hospital."

"Do you need to leave? It's slow. Colie and I can handle it..."

"No, it's fine," I say, rubbing a hand over my face. "I can't get out of San Diego until morning, anyway."

Except I'm not in the right frame of mind and working isn't doing me any good. Colie pulls me aside not even twenty minutes later.

"Honestly, Jake. Go home. It's only a half hour early. Go home, figure out how and when you're getting to your family, and we'll take care of things here."

"I can't just leave. I have thirty-six hours that need to be covered through Sunday night. So I go back to Montana just tomorrow and turn around right away?"

She frowns. "Go be with your family, Jake. Your parents would have told you if it wasn't serious and even if it turns out she's okay...you'd kick yourself if you didn't go and she *wasn't* okay. We can figure out your shifts and get them covered. Conor's in tomorrow, anyway, to do payroll because he couldn't do it this afternoon."

My head's at war with itself but she's right about one thing—if I don't go and Hollis's injuries are on the really bad side...

I once again need to remind my head not to go there.

"All right." I nod. "Okay, thanks, Cole."

"Please keep us updated. I know we don't know her but you're like family to everyone here so... Just let us know, okay?"

"I will." I grab my things and head out, prepared to get home and start packing.

EIGHTEEN

I'M STARTING to get worried.

After the wedding and festivities wrapped up around nine, I sent a text to Jake to see if he was awake yet.

Nothing.

Okay. Not a big deal. It wasn't the first time one of us texted the other and a response was hours later. Such is life when your time zones are fifteen hours apart.

But I didn't have a message from him when I woke up this morning, either. In ten hours, surely I would have heard from him, right?

Sitting on my bed, legs crossed, I hold my phone as it restarts. Maybe it needed an update or something?

Emina comes out of the bathroom, finger-combing her hair up into a bun after getting ready. We decided we were going to head out again for our last day, rather than lounge in the pool and around the resort.

"Everything okay?" she asks, grabbing her tennis shoes from where she toed them off yesterday.

I shake my head. "I don't know. Jake hasn't replied and it's not like him..."

My friend grins with a small laugh. "Give the man a break, Soph. Isn't he working ridiculous hours while we're gone, because he can't stand not being able to spend time with you? He's probably sleeping."

"It's..." I open the web browser I found for time conversion. "It's five in the afternoon in San Diego. He's gone to bed *and* woken up *and* headed in for another shift by this time."

My phone jingles as the restart completes, but still, no texts or voicemails.

Emina shrugs, moving from where she sat on her bed to put her shoes on, to one of the stuffed chairs by the desk. She opens the pastry box of goodies we grabbed from a local bakery yesterday morning. "Then call O'Gallaghers. Maybe something's wrong with his phone."

"Is that weird? Am I being too...needy? Crazy?"

"The man has told you he loves you more than once," she points out, waving a croissant around as she talks. "Call the bar."

"Pub," I mumble, looking down at my phone.

"Do you want me to call for you?"

Sighing heavily, I say, "No. I can do it." I find the contact and send it through, and while the line rings, I tell Emina, "Besides, if something bad happened to him, Ben would have called. He has your number."

Emina tears a piece of croissant as she shrugs a shoulder. "Maybe, maybe not. We hang out but it's nothing serious. I don't know that I'd be the first person he'd think to contact. If Ben called anyone, he'd have called you."

"Could've fooled me," I mutter at her description of what she and Ben are or aren't, just as the line opens.

"O'Gallaghers."

I think it's Saint? Better to not try and name the person on the other end. "Um, hi. It's Sophia. Is Jake there?"

There's a minute stall that has my heart rate skyrocketing, but then maybe-probably-Saint answers, "He flew out to Montana this morning. Did he not tell you?"

Swallowing hard, I try hard to make my words come out strong and unaffected. "No. He just hasn't been answering my texts and I got worried. That would make sense then, I guess... He's busy." Why did he go home? He would have told me if he had a spontaneous trip to Montana, right?

"One of his sisters was in an accident—" I gasp into the phone, lifting my hand to my mouth, at the unexpected news, which has Emina lifting her brows as she stares across the room, "—he wasn't really in the best frame of mind last night when he got the call. I don't know who would have a number you can use... *Hey, Saint!*" Okay, so I'm not talking to Saint. "*Do you know who Sophia can talk to? Would Ben have a number?...Is he on break?...Okay, thanks.* I'm going to put you on hold real quick and find Ben, okay?"

"Yes, sure. Thank you so much." I bite my lip when the line goes quiet, praying the call doesn't drop.

"Is everything okay?" Emina asks, concern etched on her face.

"One of his sisters was in an accident. He flew back to Montana this morning. I'm waiting for—"

"Hey, Sophia," Ben says on the other end of the phone.

"Ben. Hi."

"Cash says you're looking for another phone number?"

Suddenly, I'm bombarded with negative thoughts. If Jake wanted me to know, he would have let me know. It's not hard to text someone to say, *hey, I have a family emergency, but I'll be in touch.*

And if he's in Montana, did he talk to someone about picking Em and me up at the airport on Monday? Or in all of the commotion, did he forget that's on his to-do list?

I mean, I get it. I'm just a new girlfriend, but—

"Sophia?"

Sucking in a breath, I reground myself. "I mean, I don't wanna…" Forcing myself to calm down, I try again, "I'm just worried. I know it's only been a few days but he's always reached out and now to know this happened and he hasn't said anything. I just worry," I repeat, resigned.

"I'm sure there's a reason he hasn't reached out to you," Ben offers, although it's not incredibly helpful. "Let me put you on speaker and see if I have Chandler's number."

"Thank you, Ben." I unfold myself from the bed to grab a pen and paper, hopeful he has her number.

"Yep, here it is."

I write out the digits as Ben recites them, then write out C-H-A-N-D-L-E-R in 3D block letters to calm my nerves as we finish the call.

"I promise, Sophia," he says, "there's gotta be a reason he hasn't talked to you about it. He got back to our place around one and was out the door for the airport by four. The man was running on pure adrenaline. Give Chandler a call and I'm sure she can get you connected to Jake."

I thank him and hang up, wondering if I should have asked him about picking us up come Monday.

"Chandler?" Emina asks. She's no longer eating her croissant but simply pulling apart the flakey layers.

"One of Jake's sisters."

"Hm." She pops a piece of croissant in her mouth but

puts the rest down on a napkin, pushing it away. "I'm going to go for a walk and get a good coffee. Do you want one?"

Shaking my head—I'm already too keyed up—I decline her offer. "Thank you, though."

She gives me a hug from my side before she leaves. "If we need to cancel our plans, it's okay. It's not like we have a terrible view or anything," she adds, sweeping her hand toward the glass door that showcases a gorgeous view of forests beyond an infinity pool.

"No," I dismiss the thought. "We'll still explore. I want to explore. Besides, I can't do anything from here, and we've only got today. It's totally fine. I just need to make sure..."

"I get it." She squeezes me one more time and then I'm left alone in our room. Rolling my lips between my teeth, I reach for the paper and dial Chandler's number.

The call only rings twice before it's answered. "Hello?"

"Uhm, yes. Hi. Is this Chandler?"

"This is..." The voice sounds skeptical but then again, a strange phone number called her.

"Okay. My name is Sophia. I'm Jake's—"

"Yes!" I'm surprised by the sudden excitement in her voice. "Yes, Sophia. Jake's Sophia. One second." There's rustling in the phone and what sounds like an elevator door dinging. "If I lose you, I'll call back on this number. I'm getting on an elevator."

"Oh. Okay."

"We only have to go three stories so hopefully the call stays connected."

"All right." I'm not sure what else to say. Except... "Is... Is Hollis okay?"

"Well, she's been better." There's a dry chuckle over the line. "She just wanted to get out of her end of the semester projects, I'm sure..." The woman sounds like she's trying to keep it together.

As if comedy is the only thing keeping her from falling apart.

"Look, we made it. Awesome. Good to know." There's more rustling as if she's moving down a hall until maybe a door is opened? "Jake. It's Sophia."

I swear I hear him say, "Thank fuck," but whether he said it or not, relief immediately floods my veins.

"Soph," he says into the phone seconds later, and the clear emotion in his tone has my throat tightening. "I'm sorry. My phone died and I didn't have a charger and didn't know it until I got to the airport and couldn't power on my phone for my boarding pass at security. By the time I got through security again after getting it printed, I didn't have time to buy one, and then my layover—"

"It's okay, Jake," I cut him off. "It's okay. I was just worried when I didn't hear from you."

"I didn't think a text was appropriate when I got the news, but it was like... I don't remember. Basically the middle of the wedding stuff for you and I didn't want to call if you were actively working. And then my phone died and... shit, I'm so sorry," he apologizes again.

"Please don't apologize," I tell him, truthfully, as the severity of the situation makes my initial worry seem silly and stupid.

"I know you, though. Your head went somewhere negative."

"I mean, something negative happened," I try writing it off, but once again, Jake proves he knows me better than I know myself sometimes.

"No, negative with *us*."

There's no sense challenging the statement. "I'm

working on it."

"I know. I know, baby." His sigh is evident through the phone but I don't think it has to do with the conversation at hand.

"Is Hollis okay? Are *you* okay?"

"Okay is relative," is his initial response. "My sister was in a car accident, but you know that part, I guess. She was T-boned and her car flipped a few times, we're told. One of the responding officers came in this morning to check on her. When my parents got here at like, two, she was awake but in pain and was stable overnight, but before I got on my connecting flight, so about...God, I don't remember. Ten this morning? Nine? She started complaining about a headache and was slurring her words. I guess at first the doctors thought it had to do with pain meds or something, but it turned out to be a stroke."

"Oh my god..."

"They think they caught it in time, but they're keeping her in a coma to try and help keep the swelling down in her brain. They did something called a craniotomy and removed a chunk of her skull but said they'll put it back when the swelling goes down."

"Jake, I'm so sorry," I whisper into the phone, closing my eyes at the pure sadness coming from him and his words.

"So, we're just taking turns sitting with her right now. Only one person can be in the ICU with her at a time because of her current state. But we don't want her to be alone. I'm supposed to be napping but this waiting room is not comfortable."

"How close to your parents' house is the hospital?" I ask because maybe if it's close enough, I could convince him to try and leave for a few hours to get real sleep.

"About forty-five minutes. I don't want to..."

He doesn't want to leave.

I don't think I blame him. Forty-five minutes is too far, in the scheme of things.

"They say the first couple of days are the most important in her healing, and then once they wake her up, we'll have a better idea of long-term effects."

"Please don't take this the wrong way, but do you want me to see if Ben or someone else can pick us up from the airport on Monday? So you can stay with your family?"

"No. I'll be there."

"Jake..."

"I'll be there. I already booked the flight and will get into San Diego about an hour before you guys do. It's fine."

"Only if you're sure. Because I understand—"

"I'll be there," he repeats, and I'm not going to fight him on it.

"Okay. Is there anything I can do for you? I know I'm all the way here and you're all the way there but maybe... I don't know, can I DoorDash dinner or something?"

"No, thank you. We ordered pizzas and ended up giving them to the nurses. We're all just...waiting. I'll be sitting with Hollis overnight tonight, so if you get bored and want to text, I'll be around to answer."

"You should try and get sleep." The conversation is oddly reminiscent of the one we had on Wednesday. "But please let me know if anything happens?"

"I will. Thank you for understanding, Soph. I'm sorry—"

"Hey, none of that. I promise." The pain in his voice is causing my eyes to well up but I refuse to put my emotions on him. Not when he's already in the mindset he's in. "We're just exploring today but I'll keep my phone on. Okay?"

"All right. I'll text if anything happens."

We end the call and I blow out a breath, puffing my cheeks while doing so. What a rollercoaster of emotions.

Determined to try and make today a good one, I hop in the shower for a quick rinse and get ready for the day's excursion.

———

I TEXTED Jake pictures and comments throughout the day, but he eventually stopped responding at what would be about two a.m. his time.

Hopefully, that meant he surrendered to sleep, even if it was in a chair in Hollis's room.

Emina and I didn't bother sleeping Sunday evening; we had to get to the airport late for our one a.m. flight.

The first flight was uneventful and I'm surprised that, unlike the flights here, I managed to sleep on the initial leg.

This time when we land in South Korea, we have a terribly long layover. We learn that Incheon International offers tours—I guess long layovers aren't uncommon—so Emina and I opt for a five-hour tour that brings us to Cheongwadae and then to Tongin Market. It was nice to get a chance to see South Korea and learn about its history while experiencing its traditional atmosphere, but my mind has been back in the States with Jake and worrying about his sister.

He's kept me up to date with Hollis's prognosis, although there hasn't been much change in her status. The plan currently is to keep her in a medical coma until Monday, and if the doctors are happy with her progress, they'll start waking her up.

Again, I asked Jake if he wanted to stay—Monday

would be a big day for Hollis. But again, he said no; he'd be in San Diego when we landed.

When we board our flight to Seattle from Incheon, I message him again even though I'm pretty sure it's early morning in Montana. He didn't have the night "shift" because of his flight on Monday afternoon and would be spending all of Monday at the hospital until he had to leave for the airport.

ME:

I'll have wifi on this flight so I'll be around if you want to text.

I nap for the first three hours of this ten-hour leg, and when I wake, he's messaged me back.

JAKE:

How's the travel day going so far?

It's only been about an hour since he wrote, so maybe he's still around to respond back and forth for a bit.

ME:

Long day. Excited to be home.

Before I can turn to Emina and ask if she wants to play with the Phase 10 deck we brought, my phone lights up with an incoming message.

JAKE:

Excited to see you.

ME:

Me too. I've missed you.

JAKE:

Tell me about it. I just want to hold you for a little while…

ME:

Did you take this week off from work?

Originally he planned to work like crazy while we were gone and then take a few days off after, but I'm not sure if that was foiled by his sudden trip to Montana.

JAKE:

I have to go in on Fri. Originally had off through the wkend but am grabbing shifts from the people who helped me out

ME:

Well, I look forward to the however many uninterrupted hours i can spend with you

He doesn't respond to that so I put down my phone. "You want to play Phase 10?" I ask Emina.

The plane is dark with soft ambient lighting as many on the flight are sleeping. For those on South Korea time, it would be somewhere around two a.m. There are two other overhead lights illuminated in the premium economy cabin so even though I hate being that person, I turn on one of ours, too.

We play three rounds before we're both yawning so wide, our jaws crack and eyes water.

Giggling at us both, Emina shakes her head as she puts the deck back in the worn box. "Why is it so hard to get *good* sleep on a plane?"

She stands to put the deck in her bag that's tucked in the overhead compartment and pulls down a sweatshirt.

"You know what, I should probably go potty while you're awake." I fumble with the chair buttons until I get the leg rest down and the tray table put away, then scoot past Em.

222

I don't take long and when I walk back, Emina's still standing, stretching her arms above her head. I slip back into my window seat and resituate myself as she does the same. Before closing my eyes, I take a look at my phone to see if Jake responded yet.

JAKE:

Sorry. Doctors came in for rounds. They're happy with her numbers and her pressures look good.

JAKE:

They'll start waking her up in a couple hrs like they originally planned

JAKE:

And no I'm not going to change my flight

ME:

I'm glad they're happy with her progress. Emina and I played cards but I'm going to try and take a nap. How many hours until your flight?

JAKE:

I have to leave here in two hours

ME:

Let me know when you board?

JAKE:

Will do. Sleep well

ME.

heart emoji

JAKE:

heart emoji *heart emoji*

I smile at his response—one-upping me, I see—but leave it at that. Thankfully, sleep comes easily this time.

NINETEEN

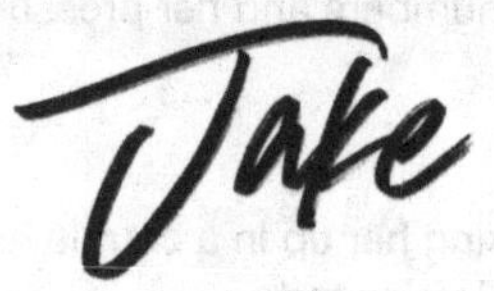

I FIND a chair in baggage claim and drop my backpack to the ground. After plopping down hard, I rub my face roughly and sigh heavily.

Knowing I'd had time to kill, I stopped at one of the gate restaurants to sit and eat a meal, although it was mostly a going-through-the-motions experience. I managed to waste nearly an hour, though. In that time, I heard from my mom. The doctors decided to delay Hollis's coma reversal until tomorrow, and they'll start first thing in the morning after rounding.

I also received an update on the Josh-situation, which, *fuck*, I haven't brought up to Sophia yet.

He had his arraignment this afternoon and as of now, hasn't made bail. I'm hoping the price is a little too steep for him and he has to sit where he's at until his lawyer talks sense into him.

The girls' flight won't land for at least another thirty

minutes, and who knows how long it will take them to get through the airport. Thankfully, they would have gone through customs in Seattle, so theoretically I don't have to wait too much longer.

Except, I must fall asleep sitting there because suddenly there's a slight jostling of my shoulder. "Jake."

I startle, more because I didn't realize I was sleeping, rather than having someone's hand on me. It takes a moment before I recover my senses and recognize where I am...and that it's Sophia standing in front of me.

"Shit," I mumble, pushing the heels of my hands into my eyes. "I fell asleep."

"I see that. You look tired." The smile on her face is soft, and *fuck*, I've missed her.

I push to stand and grab my backpack, swinging it over my shoulder at the same time I reach for her hand. She tips her face up, her lips parted, and I lean down to take her mouth with mine in a gentle homecoming kiss.

"I missed you," I whisper after pulling away, pressing my forehead to hers.

"I missed you too. Let's go home..."

It turns out, the girls came down to baggage claim and on their way to the carousel, spotted me sleeping. Soph and I head to where Emina waits for their bags.

I pay for a cart and once their luggage comes through, we stack everything and I push the cart through the airport and toward the parking garage.

"Do you want me to drive?" Sophia asks as we load their suitcases into the bed of the truck.

"I'm fine."

She lifts her brows and I give her a crooked grin. "I'm sure, Soph. I'm good."

During the trip home, I ask questions about Bali, the

job, but also their side trip in South Korea during their ten-hour layover. Both Soph and Emina tell me their stories, sometimes talking over one another, other times building on what the other said.

It sounds like an amazing trip, even if it was only a couple of days long. I tell them this and they both agree.

"We'll have to go back someday. Take more time to enjoy *and* relax," Emina says, and Sophia nods.

As I pull into the complex, I look in the rearview mirror toward Emina. "Ben texted to let me know he brought the Things back to your place before he went into O'Gallaghers at five."

"Awesome. I can't wait to snuggle and squish 'em," she answers, a small smile on her face.

I pull the truck to the curb in front of their unit and put it in park. "I'll help you guys bring your bags up but Soph, baby...I'm exhausted. I haven't gotten adequate sleep in...I don't know when. I'm just gonna go home and crash."

She doesn't respond until I'm pulling their bags out of the back. Emina's already opened the gate and unlocked the front door as I roll Sophia's suitcase away from the truck.

"Would you like me to come over?" Soph asks after lifting her suitcase over the door sill and into the small foyer.

"I'm just going to sleep."

She twists her mouth in thought, her own eyes with slightly tired bags beneath locked with mine. "I'd really like to keep you company, Jake. Even if it's just when you sleep."

And because I need her in my arms with a fierceness I've never experienced in a relationship, I invite her over.

I SLEPT HARDER than I have in a while.

There's something to be said about being with the person you love when your soul is tired.

Still, I wake at six on the dot—although I'm pretty sure I was long gone to the sleep Gods by eight-thirty, so that's the longest I've slept in one chunk since...hell, I couldn't say.

I take a deep breath in through my nose, my arms tightening around Sophia as she sleeps half on top of me.

"You awake?" she whispers. Guess she's not asleep.

"Mm. Yeah." I unlock an arm from her body to rub at my face. As I yawn, Sophia slowly drags her finger up and down my bare chest. I regrettably was too tired to have sex last night and slept in boxers while she took one of my clean shirts.

"Don't be mad at me, okay?"

Lifting my brows, I try leveling her with a look but her small smile says I miss the mark. "That's ominous," I try joking instead, my voice thick with sleep, as I secure my arms around her once more. Not concerned in the least with whatever she has to confess, I close my eyes once more, content in this moment.

"We need to go back to the airport this morning."

Pinching my brows together, I give up on rest and look in her face. "Did you forget something?"

"No. I maybe booked us flights back to Montana." Her smile is somewhere between a grimace and a *"surprise!"* expression, but then it morphs into a concerned one. "You need to be there, Jake."

"But—"

She puts her fingers over my mouth. "Even if it's just through tomorrow night. Or through late Thursday, so we're back in enough time before you need to go to work. A couple of days to be there as she's waking up and getting adjusted to her current normal. And I'm coming with you because I don't think you'd go if I didn't. I can work from anywhere so I'll just...set up shop in the hospital dining room or something."

I can only stare at this woman.

She's been away from home—out of the country—for six days and I'm sure has a ton of work to do between her normal clients and the wedding.

Yet she's doing this.

For me.

"And what if I were to tell you no?" I ask, although I'm pretty sure she knows I wouldn't.

Her face serious, she shrugs and holds her shoulder there. "Then I guess I'm meeting your family without you, because Chandler's expecting us at the airport at six tonight." Her eyes lock with mine for long moments before she takes my face in her hands and adds, "It's what you do for the ones you love."

My heart stops at her confession, even if she doesn't outright say the words. "You've been through my shit show and you're still standing. Let me stand beside you now."

I regard her with a mix of emotions. So much has happened in such a short amount of time, but one thing I know for certain—standing by Sophia's side is where I'm meant to be.

But speaking of her "shit show"...

No, I mentally shake my head. I want to hold on to this moment. It's selfish of me but I need the soft, confident version of Sophia right now.

What did I do in this lifetime to deserve a woman like her?

Unable to contain my admiration and affection for her, I

take her face in my hands and bring her closer for a kiss. A kiss she comes willingly for.

I tell her without words what I think of her decision, as her fingers gently sweep and caress through my hair above my brow.

She moans softly into my mouth, her body moving to settle more solidly on top of mine. The longer we kiss, the more I want to lose myself in her arms.

And when her core meets my hardening cock, she pulls her face away with what looks like regret marring her features.

"We board in literally three hours..."

Cocking a brow, I snort lightly. "It's been over a week since I've been inside you. I won't be lasting hours." Sliding my hands down her back, I gently grasp her bare ass, my middle fingers of each hand gliding back and forth against the crevice between the globe and her thigh. Her entire body shivers at contact. "That said, I don't like the idea of a quickie that I can't follow up with slow..." I lift my head to kiss her jaw. "Sweet..." I lick my way toward her ear, and she turns her head to allow it. "Lazy..." I nibble her earlobe gently as I slip my hands inward, my fingers now brushing her wet center. "Fucking."

Sophia whimpers, rolling her hips, trying to take more. Playfully, I circle my finger around her entrance.

"Forget what I said. I don't need hours," she pleads, her hands planting on my chest as she pushes to sit. "As long as we both come, I'm good with a quickie..."

"Then ride my cock, baby."

Together, with Soph still atop of me, we work my boxers off. She crosses her arms in front of her to pull my shirt from her body, dropping it on the bed beside us. Then she lifts her hips, scoots back a fraction, and takes me into her warm, ready heat.

"Fuck," I groan, grasping her hips. "You feel…" Fantastic. Wonderful. Slick. Warm. "*Fuck,* Soph. I'm not—"

"Birth control," she pants, lifting and slamming her body back down. "On it. Just…" Her nails dig into my chest as she rolls her hips once, twice, then starts a quicker back and forth friction.

When her head drops back, I reach up to cusp the exposed slender line of her neck, only to instead swoop to the back, pulling her down until she lays flat to me. This time when we kiss, days of pent up lust takes over. Her tits brush and jiggle over my chest and I'm torn between taking her hips in mine and pounding feverishly into her, or to take one of those breasts—particularly the left—and play until she's screaming my name. I think I'd like to do it all…

Either way, I don't have much longer before I'll be blowing my load.

Her silky walls continue to take me as she gets wetter and wetter. And regardless of the breathy moans and whimpers breaking against our kiss, I can't be positive she's *there* yet…

Sophia's the one to break our kiss though. She gasps for air as her breath stutters, small mews of pleasure accompanying the wet sounds of our fucking. Each thrust of mine is met with a high-pitched whimper of hers.

Reaching between our bodies, I scoop and push her left breast up. She arches back, allowing me to bring her tit to my mouth.

"Oooooooh," she cries softly.

I suck hard, using my mouth's suction to hold her breast to my mouth but she helps too by pushing her chest into my face. I reach back to grasp her hips once again. Sophia continues to feed her tit to my mouth, her body trembling as my tongue swirls around the peak, my teeth grazing softly only to return to teasing with my tongue.

My thrusts turn erratic, there's no more finesse as I chase my orgasm.

"Jake... God, Jake!" She screams, pulling her breast from my mouth, as her body straightens over mine, her fingernail no doubt leaving crescent moon shaped divots in my pecs.

Her entire body is tight as her orgasm courses through her body, and the way her pussy grips, loosens, grips again, fluttering around my dick, has me coming seconds later.

I grunt my release, pushing my hips against hers one last time as my cock drains into her.

Relaxed, Sophia lays on me, stretching her body around mine. Her legs straighten beside mine. Her arms reach over my head and under the pillow. She buries her face in the crook of my neck.

"I think I like quickies," she murmurs against my neck, and I manage a short laugh.

"Good to know that in a pinch, it'll still be a good time..."

"It's always a good time." She kisses my neck before moving to roll off me.

We both moan at the loss of our connection, but Soph's quickly turns into an, "Oh, shit," as she blindly reaches for the discarded shirt and stuffing it under her ass.

I can't help myself. My chuckle turns into full-blown laughter.

"It's so messy," she groans, and I can't seem to stop. She backhands my stomach, although she smiles while she makes connection.

"Here..." My moves quick, I go from supine to kneeling in seconds. "I could get you a washcloth or something," I tell her, reaching for the part of the shirt that isn't directly under her, "or we can just move into the shower." I wipe away what release I can.

"Literally a shower to clean, and then we have to get dressed, pack, and go," she warns.

"I understand we're on a time crunch," I grin. "I can behave."

And I did. It was Sophia who misbehaved, working me with a handjob before dropping to her knees to suck me off.

Handing her a towel as I get out of the shower first, I tell her, "If we're rushing through security, it's your fault."

Like the cat who got the cream, she just grins impishly, wrapping the towel around her body. "What was I supposed to do? You kept jabbing me with it and it was...*there*."

"It's often *there* when you're naked or ready to be naked," I joke right back.

She left a pair of leggings and a top here a few weeks ago, so that's what she puts on now. "I'll have to grab a sweatshirt for the plane. Remind me to, please."

I grab an extra hoodie of mine, just in case.

We somehow have enough time to walk to Sophia's, so we kill two birds with one stone and take Boo on a morning walk. We're back to mine and Ben's in twenty-minutes flat.

Boo's had her walk, she's had her breakfast, and Soph and I are both packed and heading out. The biggest problem with the time we spent this morning is parking. The lot I normally park in is mostly full and I have a feeling we'll be walking far...but luck is on our side when a car backs out just before we near.

"You want me to grab this?" Sophia asks, reaching for the charger I keep in my truck. There's the tiniest hint of teasing in her voice, and when I look at her, she winks playfully.

"Yes, please."

Because it's a quick trip, we're both packed in backpacks, which makes getting through security a breeze. While Sophia carries a laptop bag as well, she has the moving-through-security portion down pat. None of our bags are stopped for extra checking, and we're soon on our way to the gate.

We don't have to rush, but they do announce the start of boarding as we near.

It's not long before we're sitting on the plane. I offered to take the middle seat so she can have the window and not have to worry about rubbing shoulders with a stranger, but we lucked out and there wasn't a third person in our section of seats.

That's not to say I move over. I'll happily sit pressed to her side for the next however many hours.

Just as I'm putting my phone into airplane mode, I receive a notification:

YOUR MOTHER:

They're going to start waking her up. They'll reduce the medications slowly and hope she'll be breathing on her own by late afternoon. If all goes well, she'll be completely removed from the ventilator by dinner time. Maybe she'll even be completely awake when you get back!

YOUR MOTHER:

We were given a list of risks too but the doctors believe she'll be okay.

ME:

Thank you for the update. We just boarded. See you in a few hours. Love you all.

I adjust the mode and silence my phone, dropping it into the seat pocket in front of me.

When I glance over at Sophia, she's looking out the window. To give me privacy?

I reach for her hand and link our fingers together as they rest on her thigh. "You're welcome to read over my shoulder."

Her smile is part wince. "I didn't... I wasn't... So, I guess Chandler told your mom we were coming. That's good. It won't be a surprise."

Lifting our hands, I press a kiss to the back of hers before replacing them on her leg. "Are you prepared to meet everyone?"

"Oh. No." Her head moves back and forth in minute passes. "I'm not... No. Like I said, I'll just work wherever makes the most sense, and you can have the time with your family. This isn't... I mean, I'll at least meet Chandler, but it doesn't have to be a *thing*."

"Soph, baby, it's a *thing*."

As the plane reaches altitude and the announcement says we're clear to move about the cabin, I reach for the armrest between us and push it up. I barely have my arm moving around her before she snuggles into my side.

"My mom probably already has dinner ordered and scheduled to arrive at the hospital about the same time we get there," I tell her. "She's a planner like that."

"This isn't really an appropriate time, though. We can do an official meet the family later. When Hollis is better."

I'll let her have her thoughts on the subject for now, but I know that by the end of Thursday, she'll be fully within the Wesley family fold, whether she intended for it to be official or not.

"Hopefully that's sooner than later. It sounds like they hope for her to be awake by tonight."

"You said before that they'd done a craniotomy. So they just...removed part of her skull?"

"Yeah, to help with the pressure in her head."

"And they'll replace it?"

"Yes. I don't know the exact timeline. I think that's a bit further down the road but I didn't catch any of it."

Sophia reaches for a string from my hoodie and plays with it between her fingers. "It all must have been so scary."

"It was hard being all the way in California but not being able to do anything." The distance and inability to do anything triggers a thought and I mutter, "Fuck," under my breath.

Still close to me, Sophia looks up, a question on her face.

"Friday was a shitty day, even before the news of Hollis. I have an event I didn't tell you about, because you were in Bali and I didn't want you freaking out while there wasn't anything you could do. When you set up your doorbell, and you gave me permission to access it, did you connect it to your phone too?"

"Yeah, but I didn't turn the notifications on." When I glance down at her, she grimaces. "Honestly, I forgot it was there."

"Well, on Friday, Josh came over."

I'm prepared for her to push away, simply so she can process the news, but aside from frowning, she actually moves in closer. "Okay. I didn't notice anything, so he must not have broke down the door or defaced the property."

"No. I was wracking my brain, because he showed up with flowers. Do you remember him telling you he needed you for an event or something?"

"Gosh, I was so annoyed that morning, I don't remember much of the conversation."

"Well. He came with flowers, you didn't answer, he left. He did throw the flowers at the door, though. You might be able to go back and see the footage but if not and you do want to see it, I downloaded it for a cop."

Her shoulders still for a moment. "You got the police involved because he came to my door?"

"No. The police got involved because he then came to O'Gallaghers, threw shit at me, and spit at my face."

This time, she does push away from my side. Sophia's gasp is so loud, I swear the seats in front and behind us can hear it. "He did not."

"He did. Long story short, between that and then the officer finding out about Sunday morning, he was held for seventy-two hours. That was up yesterday afternoon—"

Her eyes widened frantically. "We have to let Emina know. What if he gets out and comes back? What if—"

"Baby, pause." I brush a flyaway behind her ear. "Go ahead and let her know. I'm kicking myself for not thinking of it earlier. I should have. Hell, I should said something at the airport. I'd *just* read the message from the officer. But it's been one thing after another and—"

"It's okay," she cuts me off, extending more grace than she probably should. "Your head's been all over." She reaches for her phone from the seat pocket, and connects to the plane's WiFi. "I mean, surely he's not stupid enough to keep trying but just in case... She should know."

"I agree. I'm sorry. Hopefully to ease your mind a little, I haven't been told he's posted bail and the way Friday happened, he's not allowed within 100 feet of me. Perfect scenario, he'll realize that means you, too, and he won't bother coming over. Even better scenario, he'll have a lawyer that talks sense into him and he'll realize his life is better served leaving you alone..."

"Do you think he's capable of that?" Soph asks, typing out a message and sending it quickly.

"I'd hope a guy like him wises up after being locked away for a few days. But even the officer said, typically this behavior—"

"Escalates..." She sighs heavily and, thank God, cuddles back into my side. "What a start to this relationship," she grumbles with a partial grimace, her attempt at keeping things light evident. "You sure you want to stick around? Goodness knows I'm more trouble than you could have ever asked for..."

I drop my head to press a kiss to the top of hers. "Never trouble. And I'm as positive as I've been about anything."

TWENTY

CHANDLER PULLS me in for a hug first.

At first, I keep my arms to my side, unsure what to do, but when she squeezes tighter, I return the gesture.

"Thank you for arranging this," she whispers into my ear.

Unsure what else to say, I whisper back, "You're welcome."

When the blonde, gorgeous even in sweats, female version of Jake releases me from the hug, I readjust my backpack, watching as brother and sister embrace next. Jake says something to her softly as he rubs a hand up and down her back, and soon, we're packed away in her car.

Thankfully, neither tried to get me to sit shotgun, although Jake did attempt to sit in the back with me. I'm happy sitting in the backseat, taking everything in, while the siblings take the front.

I heard back from Emina, who said she'll just be

camping out at home for the next couple of days and "won't answer doors to assholes." I re-emphasized what Jake told me and she promised she'd keep herself safe.

Listening to Jake and Chandler, it sounds like Hollis is now breathing on her own and may potentially be extubated and removed from the ventilator by the time we get to the hospital.

"Visiting hours are only until eight," she continues, putting on the car's blinker as she changes lanes, "and they were enforcing them last night. Only one of us could stay with Hollis overnight and we weren't allowed to sleep in the waiting room anymore, either. Mom and Dad grabbed a couple of rooms at the DoubleTree. I'm with Hollis tonight, so you guys can get a room to yourselves. Be warned, it does have a connecting door to Mom and Dad's."

I look out the window as they talk about the logistics of the next couple of days. While we haven't booked our returning flights yet, we'll have to leave sometime Thursday so Jake can open at O'Gallaghers on Friday. That gives us a good day and a half, which means Jake can spend a decent amount of time with his family. Even better if Hollis is awake for it.

"Jake tells me you're a video editor?"

Snapping back to the moment, I turn my head toward Chandler's seat. "I am."

"That's neat. He couldn't stop gushing about how you also took really good videos and a couple paid for you and your friend to document their wedding in Bali. How freaking cool is that?"

"I'm not the *best* videographer—"

"Don't let her fool you. She's great." Jake's whisper toward his sister is loud and exaggerated.

"...But I'm excited to put the footage together for the full video."

"When you called Saturday I was so worried the call would drop in the elevator and even though I had your number, I had this fear it wouldn't go through because you were on the other side of the world. Of course, if Jake's phone would have just charged..."

I'm not sure how to respond, so I simply offer her a smile when she glances at me in her rearview mirror.

Jake reaches an arm behind his seat and gently grabs my leg, his thumb smoothing up and down in a light caress.

It's silly, but the closer we get to the hospital—and the only reason I know we're getting closer is because Chandler's phone is propped on the dash with her GPS screen on display—the tighter my chest feels.

I'm nervous.

Frankly, I'm terrified.

What if his parents don't like me? What if they think this was the wrong time to come?

I should have just put Jake on the plane. Sent him with a hug and a kiss, and told him he'd be fine for a few more days. What was two more days after six apart?

Maybe I can just stay at the hotel tomorrow. Yeah. That'd be a good idea. Besides, Jake knows I have to work, and why lug everything into the hospital only to sit in a quiet waiting room by myself?

I can sit in a hotel room by myself.

That's what—

Jake shifts in his seat, twisting to look over the back and at me. His eyes study mine and I know he can see my mind is racing.

Because he sees everything.

He doesn't cock a brow.

Doesn't wink or do something ridiculous to get me to smile.

He simply stares at me, and the love I see in his eyes magically dissolves the worry that's no doubt behind mine.

Head calming, I offer him a small upturn of my lips and this one he returns. It'll be okay.

It will be alright.

———

BY THE TIME we get to the ICU floor, there's only fifteen minutes left for visiting hours, which the unit secretary was sure to let us know—both when she opened the unit doors by push of a button, as well as when we passed the desk she sat at.

All of the rooms are behind glass sliding doors, and most have a privacy curtain drawn, as well. When we stop in front of Room 11, the curtain isn't pulled here and I can see into the room. There are two people, whom I assume are Jake's parents, beside the bed. One standing at the head and the other sitting in a chair about midway. It looks like they're talking to Hollis, who isn't visible from this angle due to the curtain being bunched to one side of the track.

"It looks like she might be awake," Chandler giddily tells us, pulling open the sliding door. "Knock, knock. I brought visitors."

His parents look over as Chandler steps in. The moment his mom's eyes meet mine, my feet feel as if they're stuck in concrete blocks.

I haven't let Jake know my intention is to stay in the hall, but he's clearly aware that was my plan. He grasps my hand, intertwining our fingers, and leans down. "They don't bite. Promise. Hold my hand?"

I attempt to give him a comical tip of my head, but he sees right through me.

"You don't have to come in if you're uncomfortable," he says softly, leaning into my space to talk directly into my ear. "I would love for you to meet them. But if that needs to be later, it can be later."

It would be easier to stay out here.

To let him see the current state of his youngest sister, and to experience the start of a new healing journey with his immediate family.

Yet it's the fact he's not pressuring me to do what he wants that has me squeezing his hand in return.

In nerves? Fear? Or maybe in solidarity.

"Okay."

His answering smile isn't a "gotcha" kind of smile.

It's...

Relieved?

Is it possible that his grabbing my hand wasn't about comforting me, but him finding a lifeline in his own sea of unease?

God, being stuck in your own head can be so damning.

We follow behind Chandler, and while my body feels heavy with anxiety, each step becomes easier and easier.

"Look who's awake," his mom says, reaching over to take Hollis's hand from where it lay on the bed. There's such relief in her voice.

Jake's grip on my hand tightens and doesn't let up, as he attempts to tease, "Hollis, if you didn't want to see me on Saturday, you could have just told Mom and Dad to tell me to cancel my flight."

While Jake and Chandler look to be an equal mix of their parents, Hollis is their mother's carbon copy. Even with her shaved, partially depressed scalp, tubes and wires coming from all over, and cuts and scratches on her face and arms, she's beautiful.

I'm sure she's even more beautiful to these people standing around her, supporting her, because of what she's been through. She's still here.

She's still with them.

The youngest Wesley attempts a smile, and only half of her face responds. "H-h-hi," she finally manages, her voice soft and rough.

Slowly, her eyes track to me. Noticing, Jake finally releases his grip but only so he can wrap his arm around my shoulders. "This is Sophia. Sophia, this is my baby sister, Hollis."

This time when she tries to speak, nothing comes out. Her face falls in disappointment.

"She's experiencing some aphasia," Jake's dad says, brushing a hand over Hollis's head, explaining Hollis's inability to speak full sentences. "The doctors said it's where she has difficulty speaking and coming up with words, but it's to be expected due to the stroke."

"They still anticipate a full recovery," his mom adds, and her gaze is on her daughter, as if she's trying to help Hollis believe this is only a bump in the road.

We visit until Hollis's overnight nurse tells us it's time to leave. Jake bends over Hollis's bed and gives her a gentle hug. I watch as she squeezes her eyes shut and a tear falls down her cheek.

I have to look away before I'll cry, too.

Not daring to be part of this intimate moment between family, I step out of the room, waiting just outside the sliding door. I give an awkward smile to a nurse sitting at a nearby desk.

When Jake joins me, I slide my hand around his waist

and give him a reassuring squeeze. He drops his head to kiss my forehead as he sighs slowly, the weight of the last twenty minutes heavy.

"Did you guys have dinner?" Mrs. Wesley asks as Mr. Wesley closes the door behind them.

"No. Just airplane snacks," Jake replies, and I drop my arm from around him as we all move to exit the ICU.

"There's a few restaurants near the hotel, if you're hungry?"

I get the feeling Jake is about to refuse on my account and my level of comfort, but there's almost a touch of hope in his mom's words.

"I could go for real food," I answer for us. Did my voice shake? Did it come out as positive and secure as I wanted it to be? "Jake?"

When he looks at me, the range of emotions on his face nearly does me in. But it's the love I see there that assures me I made the right choice.

DINNER WAS BLISSFULLY EASY.

There was hardly any talk of Hollis, but I think that had more to do with everyone needing a moment of normalcy. Hollis's upcoming trials in healing will take enough of their energy.

Taking an hour to not worry is healthy.

They asked questions about how Jake and I met, and while he was honest about meeting me at O'Gallaghers while working, Jake left out the part where I ended up drunk off my ass. They, too, had heard about my trip to Bali, and asked questions about that.

The questions were all respectful and curious, and

while I'd never ask them to stop, Jake sensed my growing anxiety and changed the subject.

"They like you," he informs me when we're settling into the hotel room. The bed closest to the door is made but has a pillow on it that doesn't match the others. Assuming that's the bed Chandler slept in the night before, we take the other.

I unzip my backpack to pull out clothes to sleep in. "You got that from the little time we spent together?" That's not me being snarky. It's me being worried.

"That and, when I hugged my mom goodnight, she told me so."

"I like them too," I tell him honestly. With my bag zipped once more, I carry both it and my laptop bag to the room's desk, placing them out of the way.

Together, we brush our teeth and get ready for bed. I'm pretty sure I can hear the shower in the room his parents are in, *and* the television in the other room we're sandwiched between.

The walls aren't thin, but they certainly aren't thick, either.

Jake turns down the bed for us and when we're both under the covers, reaches over to turn off the single-bulb lamp. I snuggle close, pushing my leg between his in a way we often cuddle.

For once, the constant chatter in my head is silent.

"I love you," he whispers against my forehead.

I tip my head back to try and see him in the dark. "I love you too." I realize it's the first time I've actually said the words, but it feels necessary.

"Yeah?"

"Mmhm. So very much."

His arms tighten around me in a relieved hug.

"Your family... You all look so much alike."

Jake's chest rumbles as he chuckles. "Chandler hated when people in town told her she looked just like her older brother. I think Hollis got off mostly easy in comparison."

"There's still no mistaking she's your sister."

He's quiet for a moment at that, so I continue, "She has the right family behind her to make it through this chapter. I have no doubt she'll be back on her feet and finishing school, before you all know it. Your mom said she was majoring in education?"

"Yeah. Early elementary age."

"So like, kindergarten and first grade?"

"I believe so."

I may have never met her before tonight and only have the stories told by Jake to go off of, but there's little doubt in my mind of the validity in my next words. "She'll be a great one."

Jake doesn't discount it. He doesn't say she's just as likely to fail at her dream because of what's happened to her.

Because that's not the person Jake is. It's not the person his family raised him—and his sisters—to be. He's the type of guy who shines from the inside out, and when your own light has dimmed, he lets you borrow his until you've got control again.

"You know," I whisper, "I would never tell someone that their forever is on the other side of one stupidly drunk night but... I wouldn't trade that night for anything."

"Me neither, Soph. Me neither..."

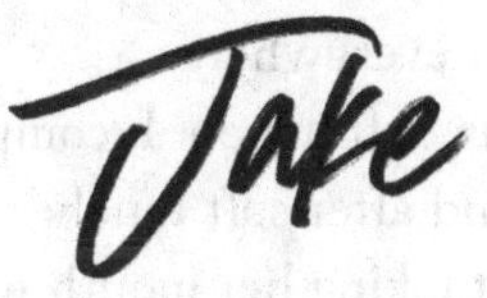

Three Weeks Later

"OH MY GOD, I'M DYING," Sophia whines, her body arching as she tries to take more than I'm giving her.

I keep my touches light, barely skimming her heated skin as my tongue all but dances around her nipple.

So.

Light.

Hardly.

Touching.

Her nipple tightens as my breath blows over, and if it weren't for her hands being tied and bound to the bed frame, I know she'd take my head and just push me onto her breast.

"You like soft touches," I remind her, giving her a tiny,

tiny bit of reprieve by flicking the very, *very* tip of my tongue barely, hardly over the distended peak of her breast.

"When I'm not already so turned on I could combust!" Her knees come up as she attempts to twist below me, trying to at least get my hips to rest against hers.

Because even my hard dick bobs so close to her skin, she can feel the nearly-there contact.

I'm hardly touching her anywhere.

Yet surround her everywhere.

Her whimper is soft when I completely move away from her breast. "And after soft touches," I whisper against her lips, but still not taking her mouth with mine, "you like to play..."

"I also like to squeeze my fucking nipple so hard I'll come the second I touch my clit but I don't see you doing that," she growls between clenched teeth.

"Lies," I tease quietly, biting her bottom lip a little harder than I normally would.

In the three weeks since we've been back to San Diego, life has been euphorically normal.

Hollis was moved to a neuro unit at the hospital and has been working hard at all the therapies—speech, occupation, and physical. While she's not 100% and probably won't be for a few more months, she's better. She's also headstrong and refuses to give up.

Sophia and I have discussed what happens when her lease is up this summer. The girls' sixty-day notification is due soon.

I'm pretty sure there's going to be some shuffling of things from one house to another, but there's still some question about what Ben's plans are.

Apparently there was some sort of falling out between Ben and Emina, but neither of them will talk about it.

Soph and I told Ben he could stay here and he laughed in our faces. *"You guys fuck all the time. Which, great for you. I just don't want to hear it."*

I about killed Ben with a look then because I *knew* Sophia was going to get weird about sex whenever Ben was home, even if it was four in the morning and he was sleeping.

It may make more sense for Soph and I to get our own place, leaving the existing leases to our roommates.

However it ends up, we're both aware it's a year-long commitment but neither of us is concerned. When you know, you know.

"If you don't fuck me..." Sophia pulls on the restraints. Those are a new addition to our playing.

Just like the entire drawer of toys—but damn, the good shit's expensive. We bought a knock-off rose toy that was supposed to flutter around her clit and nipples, and the damn thing died the first time we used it.

Plugging it in didn't work, either. It was just...

Dead on arrival.

I ease back from her body, my eyes taking in her delicious form. I can't wait to sink into her but...

First things first.

Reaching for the drawer, I take out her trusty magenta dick.

Sophia watches my moves and when I turn the toy on, she closes her eyes. "Jake..." Instead of demanding my cock, she spreads her legs wider.

Her eyes snap open to the sound of the lube lid clicking open after I retrieve that from the drawer, too.

I watch her watch the gel hit the head of the toy and after I've closed the bottle and tossed it back, I use my hand to spread the liquid around the tip of the vibrator.

"This will feel good, baby," I promise when her eyebrows raise. We don't do many insertables, and she'll tell me if it's too much.

"You better not ruin my heightened state of desire." She tries to sound badass but the words end in a moan when I run my finger down her wet folds.

Settling my body between her legs, I spread her pussy lips and prepare for the feast in front of me. Glancing up at her, Sophia has her bottom lip between her teeth, her entire body primed and ready in anticipation.

If her hands were free, I have little doubt she'd either have them in my hair or on her chest, tweaking her nipples to help her along.

Satisfied with the state of desire she's in, I lightly trace her folds with my tongue.

"Fucking damn it, Jake," she whimpers softly, her hips rolling to try and make better contact.

Hell, I could tease her body all day and all night. The explosiveness of her orgasms when she's been played and primed for an hour plus are my favorite ones to give her. I've gotten to really enjoy foreplay.

But at some point, I have to have mercy on her, and when I swirl my tongue around her clit before sucking it between my lips, her entire body relaxes as she moans loudly into the room.

I could stay here just as long as I can gently tease her nipples, but the way her breath hitches is enough of a warning that I'm running out of time.

With the lubed vibrator in hand, I bring the vibrating head to where her pussy opens. It easily notches in place and Sophia moans at the contact. Between my mouth on her clit and her body getting ready to take the girth of her toy, I know she'll come apart in seconds.

As I insert the toy, I'm gentle for reasons other than teasing her mercilessly. I don't want to hurt her by jamming the vibrator in, not when it's a toy she rarely allows to be used to fuck her with.

I stop holding her folds open so I can also play with her nipple. Between her nipple, her clit, and her pussy being stimulated by the slow push and pull of the vibrating cock within, all at the same time, I just know...

"F-f-f-u-uh-uh-ckkkk," she whimpers, her body arching off the bed as she flies apart, her body completely coming undone as the strength of her orgasm takes over. "Jake!"

This is usually the part where I sink my cock into her pulsing heat, but I have other plans for her. I angle the vibrator to try and get the head to stroke her G-spot within, milking her orgasm for all it's worth.

Eventually, her body begins to settle, but for a few full body shivers.

First, I remove my mouth from her clit.

Then, and only after a more firm caress, I release her nipple from my fingers.

I'm so hard I *ache* but I'll get mine soon enough.

Her eyes open slowly, taking a moment to focus. When those hazel orbs lock with mine, her smile is slow and satisfied.

I keep fucking her lightly with the vibrator as I lower, taking her mouth in a slow, sensual kiss. When I finally pull the vibrator from her body, it releases with a wet *pop*.

I toss it to the bed beside us before reaching up to remove her hands from the restraint, never once letting up on our kiss.

It's not much longer before she's begging to be filled again, but with my cock this time, and it's over for me in minutes.

As badly as I wanted another orgasm for her, she wouldn't let me rub her clit. Wouldn't let me go down on her again after.

"I'm more than satisfied, Jake," she mumbles against my chest, sleepy in the aftermath. "I may not be able to walk today. I think I'll just take up residence here in your bed for the day."

"Won't be coming in to watch me work this afternoon?" Nearly all of my lunch shifts, I can count on Sophia being around.

"Ugh..." She tips her head away from me so she can look in my eyes. "Ogling you while you work is so much fun though. Might have to still give it a try."

Sophia rides into town with me with a plan for Emina to come by a little later in place. Something about heading down to Lulu's for their exclusive cookie of the month tasting.

She walks in with me through the back, waiting as I clock in, before we head to the front together, splitting at the bar—I go to the back to check on my working position for the time being, and she scoots around the front to take one of the available stools.

"Hi, Colie," Sophia waves. Colie is the shift lead until two, and then I'll take over until six. Sophia and I then have a movie date at eight. Where the night goes from there, who knows.

Colie grins at my girl and then looks over at me. "You can stay up here, if you want. I've done most of the opening duties but there's an order coming in. I want to organize some of the shelves before it does."

Nodding, I grab a clean bar towel. "Not a problem."

Before she can head to the back though, the front door

opens. We both race to verbally welcome the newcomer, but Colie's "Welcome to O'Gallaghers" quickly dies on her lips as her eyes widen and her body stills.

"Liam..."

Phew. When I tell you Drunk Girl was a labor of love, I mean it. I pushed and pushed, especially after its spectacular fail in January of 2023. In that time, I struggled a lot with my head, which only got worse when my dad's cancer came back and my dog, who I've often joked is the only reason I'm here with you all today, had a health scare. And because things come in threes, a good friend who was practically the only family I have out in Arizona unexpectedly passed away around Easter.

I wanted so badly to give you all the words I've promised again and again, and here we finally are. I'm pleased with how Jake and Sophia's story turned out.

If you peek around some ebook retailers, you can quickly figure out who the next couple to be featured in this series is, but I have two other books I need to wrap up before I come back to the pub (those are Caged Lion and 82: Coast to Coast). That said, Thinking 'Bout You is up for preorder on most sites and will be available to read early/while being written for all followers on my Ream page!
http://reamstories.com/mignonmykel

Typically this is the spot where I give you the couple's "5-10 years later" epilogue (because I love them. Always. I *practically always give a decade-later update) but there's so much more to be said and done in this little corner of my world. You **will** get a look at each of these bartenders 5-10 years down the road...but it won't be until the very end.*

CAMEOS

Who did you meet in *Drunk Girl* who has a book?
Let's see...

Conor O'Gallagher — One Night Stand

The O'Gallagher Siblings Omnibus —
O'Gallagher Nights

ABOUT THE AUTHOR

Mignon Mykel is the author of the Prescott Family series, as well as the short-novella romance series, O'Gallagher Nights. When not sitting at Starbucks writing whatever her characters tell her to, you can find her hiking in the mountains of her new home in Arizona, or trying to tame her sassy (see: stubborn) mastiff-lab.

For early access to her works in progress, serialized fiction, complete access to her back catalogue, and exclusive behind the scenes previews, be sure to join her on Ream!

ALSO BY MIGNON MYKEL

Prescott Brothers

Interference

The Prequels

The Playmaker

Holiday for the Books

From the Beginning

Butterfly Save

O'Gallagher Nights

One Night Stand

About Last Night

All Night Long

Hot Holiday Nights

Enforcers of San Diego

32: Refuse to Lose

25: Angels and Assists

Back to O'Gallaghers

Drunk Girl

Douglas Group: The Protectors

Free Bird

Lone Wolf

Standalone Titles

Saving Grace

Homewrecker

Caught in the Act

Lost Without You